D1527851

CALLALOO

& Other Lesbian Love Tales

LaShonda K. Barnett

New Victoria Publishers
Norwich, Vermont

Published by New Victoria Publishers Inc., PO Box 27 Norwich, Vt.
05055, a Feminist Literary and Cultural Organization founded in
1976.

Cover Art by brendamichelle morris
Photo by S.E. Chase

Printed and Bound in Canada
1 2 3 4 5   1999   2000   2001   2002   2003

Library of Congress Cataloging-in-Publication Data

Barnett , LaShonda K., 1975-
    Callaloo & other lesbian love tales / by LaShonda K. Barnett.
            p.   cm.
        ISBN 1-892281-08-2
        1. Love Stories, American. 2. Lesbian Fiction. I. Title.
      II. Title: Callaloo and other lesbian love tales.   III. Title:
      Callaloo.
    PS3552.A6986C35   1999
    813'.54--dc21   99-25696
                                            CIP

Throw it away. Throw it away.

Give of your love, live your life, each and everyday.

And keep your hand wide open,

Let the sun shine through,

'Cause you can never lose a thing if it belongs to you.

—*Abbey Lincoln*

(*with permission from Verve*)

For Kate

Acknowledgments

I grew up in a home where my mother often chided me with "dare to be different!" Though I am sure at the time neither of us knew how different I'd turn out to be, I am grateful I grew up subconsciously knowing whatever I chose to do and whoever I chose to become, I would be loved. Thank you for this special kind of knowing, Mama.

Diana Jones provided a great source of inspiration by giving me an engraved Watermen pen, trimmed in 18 carat gold, along with a note that read: "for your future book signings." ("Velvet," your words encourage me always.)

The following people have been my harbingers of hope, especially my sister Lisa Long, who invokes the humor and honesty necessary for my survival and Vicki Zeritis, who faithfully extends emotional support—always. (This is a mother's love.) By listening to these stories, reading them or simply asking "how's the writing going?" I am thankful for the presence of many: my family, Jacki Bookshester, April Reynolds, Malinda Walford, Alicia Fritz, Rachelle Sussman, Kyes Stevens, Susan D'Aloia, Arissa White, Paula McIntire, Lisa Herod, Charlie Lott, Marion Merritt, Lisa C. Moore, Elaine Marshburn, Dana Boswell, Pat Brodsky, Patricia Mickey, Blanche White and Mary Porter. Thank you Narissa Bond for the tenderness, the lessons, and other gifts you gave along our journey. I am better for having known you.

In awe, still, I thank brendamichelle morris for creating the cover art. It amazes me that she conceived what I could not articulate. Thanks also to the many people who attend public readings and booksignings thereby reminding an author why writing matters!

At the 1998 National Women's Music Festival Catie Curtis asked me to read one of my short stories during her set. Following her performance, the publishers of this book approached me with interest in my work. Catie, thank you again for the sudden gift of fate.

Beth Dingman, Claudia McKay and Rebecca Béguin gave stellar performances in their roles as editors and publishers, for this I extend my infinite gratitude. Thank you also for your dedication and service to the world of feminist, lesbian publication.

Finally, I extend my sincerest appreciation to my Higher Power. Thank you for the gift and thank you for abundance! I am learning to accept ALL of the goodness.

Love Scenes

The Homecoming of Narda Boggs

Texas, 1959

"Ain't nothin' wrong with a little skinny dippin' Jeannie-Mae. Com' on. It's late and it's real dark out too. Them folks ain't fixin' to get out they beds—even if they do hear somethin' kinda' strange. Besides, I been Mister Boggs yard help for three summers now. I'm like one of the family. 'Bout the wurs thing he could do if he caught us naked in his pool would be to tell our mamas. But he ain't gon' do that, 'cuz he ain't gon catch us. Now com' on Jeannie-Mae. I thought you said you ain't 'fraid of nothing."

"I ain't afraid of nothing Booker Thomas Williams. But I do got the sense God gave me and this ain't right, I tell you. This just ain't right."

The light in Booker's eyes faded as he realized I was not about to take off my clothes and jump in some white man's pool. I knew Mister Boggs far better than Booker. Now grant it, he could be real friendly to his colored help but he still wouldn't take too kindly to colored people skinny dippin' in his pool.

Booker picked up the towels he'd laid on the ground near the tall iron fence by Boggs's pool and started down the path to our neck of the woods. Booker and I had been courting for three years. Every time he didn't get his way he'd pout. Tonight would be no different. I'd get the silent treatment during our walk home.

"What's the matter Booker? Cat got your tongue?"

"No."

"Then what's wrong wich you?"

"I'm tired of being poor. And being colored sure is inconvenient at times. How come we can't have a pool?"

"'Cause your mama and daddy barely make enough to keep a roof over your head." I swear that boy could ask some dumb questions.

"We don't even got a swimming pool in our neighborhood, Jeannie-Mae. It just ain't fair."

"You're right Booker. It ain't fair. Life ain't fair. Watcha' gon do about it? I'm going to college when I graduate."

"College? College?" Booker repeated with more wonderment the second time he said it. Booker always repeated his words when he was about to make fun of something.

"Yes, college," I said, determined that I would not let him make fun of my dream.

"What you gon' study in college? Home arts? Cooking, sewing, cleaning house, that's about all they don learnt you how to do in our school."

"That ain't true. You know I don took other classes. Most of my classes been English classes. I happen to like English."

"Girl, you can't even talk right. How you gon' study English? And what college gon' let you in anyway? Unless you plan on working in the cafeteria."

"For your information Booker Williams, you ain't gotta talk right to study English. Besides, you saying that talking white is talking right? Umphh. Well, I like reading literature. I'm not fixin' to study no grammar. I want to study literature and poetry. I'm gon' be a poet one day."

"Jeannie-Mae you ain't got the sense God gave a fly. How you gon' write correctly if you can't speak correctly?"

"If you paid any attention in Miss Wilson's class you would know that poets have their own language. I ain't gotta talk like everybody else. I'll make people appreciate my language."

"You think they gon' understand it?"

"You do."

Searching for a word, any word, to start an argument but finding none, Booker kicked every rock and dirt patch that met the toe of his shoe. "Guess you got a point."

I couldn't believe it. I'd shut Booker Williams up.

"Don't forget me when you get famous," he added.

We made a right turn onto my street. He kissed me good night on the porch. On his way down the porch steps he stopped. "Don't forget tomorrow they having a picnic in honor of Mister Boggs's daughter's homecoming."

"I didn't know Boggs had a daughter. Where she been? What's her name?"

"You know 'bout as much as I do." Booker said as he continued down the path.

The following day at school, Booker and I sat under my favorite dogwood. He suggested we have a picnic so we combined our lunches and shared. I was shocked that he'd come up with such a romantic idea. Then he ruined it by telling me he'd read it in some magazine while he was at the barber shop waiting for his turn in the chair.

We made bets on how we thought Mister Boggs's daughter looked. Booker imagined her short and fat like her daddy with long blonde hair and blue eyes like Mrs. Boggs. I said she was probably tall and skinny with her daddy's dark eyes. Booker told me if he was right I'd have to bake him an apple pie. And I told him if I was right he would have to make me something special in his wood carving class. We were both wrong as two left shoes.

Boggs's yard overflowed with people, plenty of food and loud music. I anxiously asked around for the mystery daughter. No one had seen hide nor hair of her. I walked over to where Booker stood and listened while he, CJ and Roosevelt—two of Boggs's yard men—talked about the world championship. Every colored person in our neighborhood, 'cept Booker and me, had crowded around somebody's radio the night before to listen to that boxing match. Roosevelt imitated Ingemar Johansson's right hook, called "The hammer of Thor," and CJ pretended he was former heavyweight champion Floyd Patterson and fell to the ground. CJ was getting off the ground, checking his pants for grass stains when a striking brown-skinned woman entered the yard. A hush fell over everybody.

In his loudest voice Boggs began, "Ladies and Gents please allow me to introduce my daughter." I couldn't help but get wide-eyed. Booker's mouth flew open.

"This is Narda Boggs. Now, I know ya'll know she ain't Maureen's daughter but her mama was very dear to me and I jes' found out she existed." He paused long enough to retrieve his handkerchief and wipe sweat from his bald spot. "We plan to take good care of her and we hope ya'll join us in this endeavor by making her feel we'com."

People started clapping—probably for lack of something better to do. Booker started acting really silly like he does every time a new girl moves into our neighborhood. I just watched her.

Later on when Booker and I were fixin' to leave the picnic, Narda approached me and introduced herself. She asked me if I attended church and if so which one. I told her that along with most of the colored folks in Beaumont, I attended Zion Grove Church of God in Christ. She said she asked 'cause before her mother's death, the two of them went to church every Sunday. She wanted to continue their tradition. Booker invited her to come along with us.

At first I was furious with Booker 'cause the only time he went to church was Easter Sunday. But at least he was brave enough to invite her, I felt very shy around her. I'd never seen anyone or anything that pretty in all my life. I couldn't help but stare at her. It didn't seem to bother her none. She was probably used to people carrying on over her, making a fuss over her looks. Maybe she was even stuck on herself, I thought. So, I turned my head to look at Booker. She thanked Booker for the invitation and told us she'd see us in church Sunday.

> "At the cross, at the cross
> where I first saw the light
> And the burdens of my heart rolled away.
> It was there by faith, I received my sight.
> And now I am happy all the day."

I fanned myself with a church bulletin as I sang along with the rest of the congregation. All the while, I'd been looking around for Narda. Between Sunday school and morning-service I went outside to search for her. Maybe she thought it was too hot to come to church. It felt like it was already a hundred degrees and it wasn't even eleven o'clock yet.

Reverend Brown told us to open our Bibles to Romans, chapter seven. Bible-less Booker took mine and found the passage. I continued to search the pews for Narda. When Reverend Brown asked us to join him in reading the scripture, from the east window I saw a person dressed in bright purple walking towards the church. As the person moved closer I was able to make out a hat with two long braids. Narda had worn that hat the day before at her homecoming. A few seconds later the door creaked open. Folks continued reading along with Reverend Brown. I didn't want to disrupt my row but I also didn't want Narda sitting alone so I waved my arm until she saw me. An usher led her to where Booker and I sat.

"Hello," she whispered to me.

"Hello. I'm glad you made it."

Sister Mabel shhed us. A 'shhh' from that woman sounded like the hiss of a snake. She know all that wasn't even called for. I rolled my eyes at her.

Narda put two pieces of butterscotch candy inside my hand. I knew one was for Booker but part of me wanted to eat mine and hold on to the other one as a keepsake. Booker greedily held out his hand.

I couldn't tell you what Reverend Brown preached about. Couldn't pay attention to anything besides Narda. I watched her out of the corner of my eye the whole service. She sat still. I enjoyed all the scents she brought with her: flowers—she probably used a little rose water behind her ears—coconut hair oil and butterscotch. The announcement of the benediction came like an unwanted surprise. Seemed like Reverend Brown ended service early.

The middle of June brought graduation from Beaumont

High School. I graduated with distinction. Booker graduated by the grace of God. Even though Mama increased my chores a bit, with school no longer in session, I had more time to spend with Narda. During the week, Booker worked at Boggs's flour plant while Narda and I ran errands for my mama, went on long walks, and talked about her life—mostly her dead mama.

Narda's mama, a Cherokee and Negro woman from Idaho, met Mister Boggs while she was passing through Texas on her way to Mexico. She planned to go to Mexico to take pictures and become a journalist. She and Boggs fell in love. When she got pregnant with Narda she was too afraid so she just ran away. Not afraid of what he'd do, mind you. Afraid of what he wouldn't do. She thought he'd stop loving her, break her heart by denying his child. Sad thing about it is she was probably wise in running away 'cause I ain't never seen no white man and colored woman living as husband and wife even though it's a lot of children 'round here that look like they're a mix. When her mama died Narda learned about Boggs and used the little bit of money she had to travel to Beaumont.

Sadness seemed to hang on to Narda. I tried to make her talk. 'Cause my Big Daddy told me that when you lose something you love the only way to heal is to remember the love. You remember the love in the telling of the love. So, I encouraged her to tell me all the stories about her mama that she could remember.

On Saturdays Booker, Narda and me would sneak and skinny dip in Boggs's pool. My first time skinny dipping seeing Narda naked excited me much more than seeing foolish Booker. I felt guilty. I mean, after all Booker had been my boyfriend for three years. I was kinda shy so me and Narda took our bathing suits off once we were inside the pool. Not Booker though. That fool undressed and had the nerve to strut out on the diving board. I thought I would die laughing 'cause for some reason I'd always imagined Booker's thing larger than it was. Narda laughed too. I swam underwater and kept my eyes open.

One Saturday, after we'd said good night and started on our way home Booker said "You sho' spend a lot of time under water. I think you like looking at Narda's body 'cause you ain't looking at me. I'm teaching myself how to dive and you act like I'm not even there."

"You're a fool," I told Booker. "Why would I be looking at some woman's body? I'm a woman myself, ain't I?"

"I don't know. Is you?"

"What's that suppose to mean?"

"Well, I don't know Jeannie-Mae. It's just that you been acting diff'rent ever since Narda became our friend. You always wid her. You always talking 'bout her. If you ain't talking 'bout her —you ain't talking. Your head is always under the water. Maybe you ain't no real woman. Maybe you what they call a bulldyker."

"What in the hell is a bulldyker?" I asked, knowing full well I knew the definition. Booker didn't answer me. By this time we were at my house. Upset that he could use such an ugly word with me, I gave him a hurried peck on the cheek and went inside.

We never talked about that night again. I stopped swimming with my head underwater. I even pretended like I heard noises by the pool's gate and told Narda we should start wearing our suits. The summer days went along without another mention of that word.

The morning my folks and me were leaving for Prairieview, where I was going to college, Narda brought me flowers in a pretty blue vase for my dorm room. We went for a walk while my daddy loaded up the truck with boxes of my books and clothes. She told me how much she'd miss our walks, our long talks, swimming with me, and going to church with me. I made her promise to write me. On the way back to the house I asked Narda if she knew what a "bulldyker" was. She said she'd heard the word but didn't care much for the way it sounded. I told her that I thought it meant a woman who loves another woman— a woman that loves a woman like a man loves a woman.

"I think I'm one then," she said. "'Cause I feel like I love you Jeannie-Mae. I feel like I love you like a man should love a woman. Do anything for you. Wish I could marry you."

Without thinking I kissed her right on the lips. She hugged me tightly.

When we got back to the house Booker was waiting on the

porch with Mama and Daddy.

"You want me to ride wid you, Jeannie Mae?" he asked.

"We got room for one more," Daddy added, proud that he'd packed the truck so well.

I looked at Narda and saw a new sadness appear on her face.

"Well, I was hoping Narda could ride with us," slipped right out of my mouth.

Mama saved the day. "I don't see anything wrong with that. Booker you can ride down with me later when I visit Jeannie-Mae. Why don't you run and tell Mister Boggs that Narda's gon ride with us. Tell him we'll be safe and bring her home proper, before nightfall," Mama said.

Booker hugged me goodbye and went on his way. Narda and I climbed in the back of the truck. Daddy helped Mama inside before climbing in and the four of us were on our way.

Rituals

Nella leaned back in her second-hand rocking chair as she wiped sweat from her brow with the back of her wrinkled black hand. The old porch squeaked each time she rocked forward. Nella watched two light-skinned boys kick a tin can back and forth between them in the middle of the road and wondered how late in the day it was getting to be.

Muriel, Nella's friend, sat on the same porch in a relatively new wicker chair with bright floral pillows neatly placed behind her small back. Muriel looked at her watch and told herself it would soon be time to wash and snap the green beans and set the fat-meat to boiling for her and Nella's supper.

Muriel's long wavy hair fell loosely on her shoulders beneath a wide-brimmed straw hat. Her reddish-brown-skin, Nella sometimes called her "nutmeg," was shining from the olive oil she religiously rubbed on her face to decrease her chances of getting too many wrinkles.

Nella's short coarse hair was parted down the center. Two separate plaits started at the front of her forehead and ended by her ears. Tiny tight gray curls, too short to braid, outlined her taut black face. She wore no hat. Both women were old. Both women had been young once and in love with each other. Their youth had escaped them—their love had not.

Nella often thought about the future, aging, while Muriel reminisced about the good ole' days—dancing to jazz music and Friday night fish fries with Jimmie and Gradie, those exquisitely dressed and extremely debonair sissies that'd looked out for her and Nella when they'd first come to Alabama. Thinking and reminiscing was their daily ritual.

Nella always found something young to stare at while she thought about growing old. Usually, it was an inanimate object, like a blooming flower. Today it was two young boys who kicked a noisy tin can between the two of them in the middle of the road.

Muriel fixed her eyes on Nella and smiled. I hope you want green beans, corn bread, and fat-meat tonight—'cuz that's what I'm in the mood for, Muriel thought; although the menu was subject to change if Muriel doubted for a second Nella wouldn't be pleased with it.

Over the years Muriel and Nella fed each other everything; comfort, home-made biscuits and gooseberry jam, passionate lips, understanding, collard greens, eager fingers, encouragement, ripe plums and green bananas, slippery tongues, advice, rich tapioca pudding, and love. Muriel delighted in her daily ritual of preparing meals for the two of them. Nella enjoyed eating whatever Muriel prepared.

The young boys stopped kicking the noisy tin can when they heard a woman's voice call out, "time to eat." Nella glanced over at her lover of forty-seven years and thought green beans, corn bread, and fat-meat sound jes' fine. Jes' fine. The two smiled at each other in silent appreciation of their rituals.

But Beautiful

Lilah enjoys thinking of phases of her life as film shorts—until now, perfect material for an average melodrama. But, after her recent move to Richmond, her discovery that love has entered her life again (after she deemed this both implausible and impossible), and her struggle with this discovery, makes her hopeful that this phase might last long enough to be a feature film.

At the beginning of this new movie, the camera pans to an interstate 64 sign before focusing on a Volkswagen Jetta that briskly makes its way down the highway toward New York. It's a quarter to eight in the morning. Lilah cruises at 70 miles an hour with a duffel bag of clothes in the passenger's seat, a McDonald's Egg McMuffin balanced on the napkin spread across her lap and a jazz tape playing to keep her company. Friends expect to join her in the Bronx around three pm. "I'll make it on time," she says to the empty car while her mind flashes scenes of a nightmare rush-hour in Washington D.C. or a crazy traffic-jam on the George Washington Bridge in New

York. This scene is cartoon-like with a Godzilla or King Kong-like creature, bending, picking up cars and placing them on top of skyscrapers so Lilah can go on her way expediently. (Some people in the audience would laugh at this. Not necessarily because it's so funny, but because they identify with the desire to be omnipotent during bad traffic.)

First flashback scene: The peaceful two-lane highway from Lilah's home town to Richmond stretches out between gargantuan trees. Traveling that route she has witnessed skies a perfect azure mingled with cirrus clouds or midnight blue with a perfect smattering of stars. On that road she has always feels safe. The trees are comforting. They resemble female soldiers standing guard making sure she passes through this place safely.

Second flashback scene: She is moving into an apartment and starting a graduate program in Richmond. On day two or three of her new life she notices an attractive woman, but before allowing herself to give any thought to this woman as a "potential," she reminds herself that she is not ready for (or is it worthy of?) a relationship. Besides, this woman is white and probably straight.

A week passes. After several intense days of unpacking, orientating herself to her new town, and second-guessing her abilities, Lilah searches for where the girls are. On a very lonesome Friday night the thought, surely there are lesbians in the Commonwealth of Virginia, implodes within her while she stands in front of the bathroom mirror.

Pulling out of her apartment complex she sees the woman again—the white woman, who is probably straight. She slows the car and rolls the window down because the woman looks bewildered. "Aren't you in my graduate program?" Lilah asks.

The woman answers, "yes" and appears awfully grateful to have had this question posed to her. Her gratitude is revealed by the fact that she volunteers more information. She explains that she's just called a cab to take her to the movie theater.

Lilah decides to go out on a limb and says, "I'm in search of lesbian ener—"

Before she can finish the word the woman is in the car. Lilah notices her Smith College sweatshirt. While pulling onto the street, she opens the sun roof and cranks up the stereo. Nanci Griffith tunes greet the night skies. The woman compliments Lilah on her music and starts singing along at the top of her voice, very passionately, very off-key. Lilah smiles.

They arrive at a bar and dance to all the fast tunes. During the slow songs they swap stories. The woman's (Kelsea is her name) stories make Lilah laugh long and hard—the type of laughter that heals old wounds and leaves you wanting more.

Their night ends with a hug because Kelsea is so "grateful" that Lilah did not pass her by in the parking lot.

The third scene is full of so much fun stuff it goes by in a flash. Two women talking hours on end. Two women buying groceries and cooking together. Two women studying together. Two women discussing the world together. Two women shopping together. Two women going to concerts, movies, the gym, the library, everywhere together. Two women leaning on each other. Two women helping each other. Two women spending so much time together they can't remember the last time they spent a day apart. Two women falling in love.

The fourth scene is not happy. It if full of difficult dialogue and much soul searching for Lilah. In this scene the audience receives visual clues that the leading lady is tormented. After hearing a journal entry spoken aloud in her head the audience understands that Lilah feels she is breaking her rule by dating and falling for a white woman. She thinks what many Black women have affirmed for her—that it: "...never works out." "It may be fun for awhile but inevitably you want, need, have to have a sistah."

She drops her pen when she considers her kinfolk. "They will die," she thinks out loud. A picture of her mother and aunts Birdie and Josephine in three caskets being lowered into the ground on the same sad, sad day, pops into her head. (The audience laughs.) Lilah knows that while a triple funeral will probably not occur, "What is she doing on the arm of that blue-eyed heffa? Bad enough she ain't going with Black men. Damn. Can't she find a Black woman?" and other hurtful verbiage will fly behind her back, turn corners and spill into her ears and heart—accidentally on purpose. She can't do it, she convinces herself.

She puts on her scholar's cap remembering the painful lessons she received along with her undergraduate women's studies degree. "Damn, I must be going crazy," she says directly into the face of the camera. She recalls lectures on white nineteenth-century suffrage groups who denied Black women participation. She recalls lectures on twentieth-century second-wave feminism where feminists embraced fear instead of discussing issues of race and class. She recalls moments of feeling utterly helpless and totally unrepresented in the classroom. She decides that this woman will give her empathy instead of true understanding and will exoticize her instead of recognizing her as fully human. She can't do it, she convinces herself. The scene ends with Lilah ignoring phone calls from Kelsea, even erasing messages left on her machine by Kelsea before listening to them all the way through.

Scene five is dramatic. The camera does a close up of Kelsea angrily hurrying to Lilah's apartment. She bangs on the door. Lilah answers. Kelsea tells Lilah she has missed her, that she doesn't understand why none of her calls have been returned or why Lilah now runs away after their classes are over. Lilah covers up the fact that she does not feel ready for (or is it worthy of?) a relationship with excuses. But she is happy to see Kelsea, so when Kelsea suggests they go dancing, she agrees.

At the bar they order drinks before a very strained conversation ensues. Kelsea asks, "Have you ever dated a white woman before?"

Lilah answers crudely, "I've fucked one. Two. Some."

"Wrong answer or maybe my question was wrong. Have

you ever loved a white woman—considered a white woman your partner?" Kelsea asks.

"No."

"You're too political for that?"

Lilah allows fear to speak for her. "It's not about being political. It's about saving myself from heartache. Inevitable disappointment."

Kelsea is offended and hurt. Hurt because Lilah has just labeled her a 'disappointment.' She replies, "It's about fear."

"Fear?"

"Fear. It must be about fear because I would never ask you to rethink, reevaluate history as you've experienced it. But, I'd expect you to treat me as an individual. I hope you won't expect me to apologize for who I am because learning to be me has been harder than you know. You're afraid—afraid that you won't be able to relate to me without falling back on your expectation that I'm going to let you down because I'm white. And you know what? I don't want to be with a coward. I don't want to be with anyone who will chalk up all of my actions, all of my mistakes to the fact that I'm white."

On that note, Kelsea downs her beer. Lilah looks away. Their dialogue stops. The dj announces "last song" and Lilah struggles to find the right words to apologize for an offense influenced by fear.

Kelsea recognizes the beginning of "To Make You Feel My Love" and extends her hand to Lilah. Lilah takes it, stands up and follows her to the dance floor. Lilah is not a Garth Brooks fan but tonight she loves him. They hold each other tightly and this scene fades to the next.

Scene six focuses on the conversations of Lilah and Kelsea. Their conversations not only include stories of success and dreams that came true, but also defeats and the dreams that didn't make it. Their conversations don't just attest to all that has gone right in their lives, but the moments when things went wrong, terribly wrong, and what they wouldn't give to right those wrongs. (This is the part in the movie when everyone in the theater knows this is real love.)

Having passed through D.C., Maryland and Delaware, Lilah stops to get more gas on the New Jersey turnpike. The trip has gone by fast. When she returns to the road she returns to organizing the scenes. She decides the "love scene" will be tastefully done and very, very short because after all the whole story has been about love—discovering it, feeling worthy of it, owning it.

The love scene follows Lilah and Kelsea's dinner at a nice French restaurant. The two stand inside Lilah's apartment. Kelsea kisses Lilah. The camera zooms in on their lips. Lips together for moments that seem to transcend all measurements of time. (The audience needs no more. After such a kiss they can dream about what follows.) The camera fades into the next scene which switches the audience back to the present.

Lilah recalls what followed that kiss as she nears the

George Washington Bridge. (The audience knows this recollection is a favorable one by her smile.) Cassette three or four flips sides. The smoky-timbred, never-faltering voice of Betty Carter fills the car:

> Love is funny or it's sad
> Or it's quiet or it's mad
> It's a good thing or it's bad but beautiful
> Beautiful to take a chance
> And if you fall, you fall
> And I'm thinking, I wouldn't mind at all.
> Love is tearful or it's gay.
> It's a problem or it's play.
> It's a heartache either way.
> But Beautiful—
> And I'm thinking, if you were mine I'd never let you go.
> And that would be but beautiful, I know.*

Lilah stops the tape. In search of a pay phone, she takes the nearest exit. She pulls into an Amoco station, digs in her purse for a calling card and gets out of the car. She runs to the pay phone and dials Kelsea.

Kelsea answers.

"Hello," Lilah begins anxiously.

"You made it already?"

But beautiful, Lilah repeats in her head. But beautiful, but beautiful, but beautiful replaces the old "I'm afraid" mantra.

"Hello? Hello? Lilah are you there?" Lilah hesitates before speaking words she hasn't uttered in a long, long time. "I love you," she softly pronounces into the phone.

Kelsea is silent and then says, "I need your love—I want your love." She pauses. "And I love you too."

The final scene shows Lilah returning to the car where she rewinds "But Beautiful" She turns the volume up a bit and races into her future, her happy ending.

Camera fade to black. "This film is lovingly dedicated to the memory of jazz great Betty Carter, 1929-1998. Thank you Betty for singing the only words that could describe the feelings of Lilah Barnes.

---

*"But Beautiful" was written and composed by Jimmy Van Heusen and Johnny Burke in 1956.

Miss Hannah's Lesson

Louisiana, 1850

"Comment vous appelez-vous?"

"Je m'appelle Sarah."

"Où habitez-vous?"

"J'habite à Dubbonnet. J'habite près de Baton Rouge."

The young woman closed the leather bound book and slowly raised her head until their eyes met.

"You are doing well Sarah, I do not understand why my people consider your people inferior. Your facility for language is exceptional. French is a difficult language, yet you show quite an affinity for it. I am proud of you." The teacher's taut expression transformed to a warm smile.

When Miss Hannah spoke, her enunciated words were soft and seemed to have a mesmerizing effect on her pupil, Sarah. Sarah enjoyed her secret meetings with Miss Hannah beyond words; mostly because Miss Hannah would sneak fresh buttered biscuits from breakfast that Sarah had prepared.

The idea of being sold to another plantation or the thought

of being married off with the sole purpose of producing more slave-hands horrified Sarah. Eighteen years on this earth had given her strife and tremendous heartache. The only joy she'd known was in Miss Hannah's presence. This was obvious to anyone who beheld the two. Sarah hung on every word said, uttered or faintly whispered by her mistress.

Her devotion to Miss Hannah was far beyond the understanding of the other house nigras and field-hands. Sarah once overheard Clara, the main cook for the Big House say, "It's not natural for dat gurl to enjoy the company of a white woman so much. She acks like a hungry newborn baby and Miss Hannah is de only one wid da tit to feed her. She never talk wid gurlz her own age or her own kin'. Cuz she pretty wid long hair she tink she white, but she ain't. I certainly hope Miss Hannah ain't tellin' dat gurl she white. Sarah fool enuf to believe it."

That instant Sarah realized prejudice stems from people not understanding what is different from themselves.

"We look different," she told Miss Hannah one afternoon during one of their secret meetings. "That's why white people hate us. I don't believe they think we're all lazy and ignorant. It is just because we're different."

She then stood and walked over to the broken piece of mirror propped in the corner of her small, dilapidated room. She motioned for Miss Hannah to join her. The two stared at their reflections. Sarah turned to face Miss Hannah who, although small, had a strong body comparable to that of a healthy adolescent boy. Using her index finger, she traced the bridge of her teacher's short, thin nose. Then she lifted Miss Hannah's hand and placed it on her own caramel-colored face. Miss Hannah traced the round nose and allowed her fingers to delicately glide along the contours of Sarah's plum-tinted lips.

Miss Hannah had herself been reprimanded by her father for taking such an interest in a nigra. "Dear Lawd, why have you given me a thirty-year-old spinster daughter who loves being around a nigga-gal?" he had yelled in a fit of rage one evening after supper. "Hannah, I absolutely forbid you to continue being seen with her."

Miss Hannah paid particular attention to her father's final words, "Being seen with her" became that clause she would heed.

After her father's order, Miss Hannah disappeared every afternoon between the hours of one and three. She made sure Sarah would not be needed in the Big House those hours by giving the other house nigras candies, meats, fragrances and sometimes shiny coins if they did Sarah's share of the work.

Their secret meetings had begun with etiquette lessons. In her presence, Miss Hannah absolutely forbade Sarah to eat with her fingers. "You are not an ape," She vehemently spat at her one afternoon. "From now on you are to use these," She pulled a knife, spoon and two different-sized forks from her handbag. Sarah immediately recognized them as part of the Big House's finest silver.

"If anyone finds these here they'll think I stole them," Sarah worriedly replied.

"We'll keep them in a safe place," Miss Hannah concluded. And so they did. The silver remained undiscovered, wrapped in a towel between one of the floor boards under Sarah's writing table and the fertile soil of the plantation. After teaching Sarah to eat properly, sit and walk like a true woman, she taught her to read and write. The two read from the Holy Bible. After having read the entire Bible—this took over three years—Miss Hannah had asked Sarah which book she enjoyed most.

"Psalms," Sarah proudly answered.

"Why?" Miss Hannah asked.

Sarah, ashamed of lying, softly spoke. "I don't know why."

She withheld the honest answer to her teacher's question for fear of her reaction. Had her fear not existed, Sarah would have explained that she likened herself to the young David who sang the most beautiful praises unto the Lord. And if she could, she too would sing similar praises unto Miss Hannah.

Now Miss Hannah was teaching her to speak French and was very pleased with Sarah's progress. "Sarah may I ask you a question? It may be indelicate, yet I feel it worthy of discussion."

"Of course Miss Hannah." She listened eagerly and prayed she might give a respectable answer.

"Have you laid with a man?"

Sarah hesitated for she did not want to disappoint Miss

Hannah in any way. She looked down at her lap and whispered, "Yes ma'am."

"How old were you?"

"Thirteen," she answered looking at the faded flowers on her best apron.

Sarah had been thirteen when she began working as Clara's kitchen-aid, Miss Hannah recalled. This recollection caused her to wonder if her father or perhaps a regular visitor to the Big House was the perpetrator.

"Who was that gentleman?" Hanna asked.

"I do not know his name." Sarah answered as she looked into her teacher's mournful eyes.

"It still happens?"

"Yes."

"Who is he? When do you have time? Where does it happen? Do you love him?" Miss Hannah's voice grew louder as she became more distraught.

"For five years I have been with your father's friend—the shrimper from New Orleans. When he comes to Dubbonnet, your father orders me to meet him at a house near the river front. When I return, I come with shrimp, and fish for the Big House. So it appears that I went to the river front to fetch food. I also bring money for your father. The shrimper comes at the end of each month. I have been with him each time except last month. Last month I started to bleed early." Sarah paused before answering the last question. "No. I do not love him."

"Why have you not become pregnant?" Miss Hannah's voice cracked when she spoke. Tears welled in her small sapphire eyes.

"I don't know. Perhaps because I pray every night that the Lord will not bless my womb with children. To live each day afraid that my child might be torn from me, sold like chattel, taken away to another plantation would be a grief that would surely kill me. I never want to bear children. I pray. I pray and dream. I dream of leaving this place, going far, far away. Though I know my feet cannot carry me far enough from the cries, the pain, the heartache I have known here."

"What would you do—at this faraway place?"

"Sew. I love sewing. I love using my hands. I am glad when I have made something beautiful. I would sew only for appreciative people. I loved sewing for your mother. She always praised my work."

Miss Hannah thought of her deceased mother and remembered how kind she'd been. Because of Tressie, Sarah had never known the hardships of field labor or the pain flogging. Tressie had taken an interest in Sarah after Sarah's mother, her favorite servant, died during child labor. At seven years old, under Tressie's care, she had received instruction in sewing. Miss Hannah's mother was a genuinely good person miscast in her part of a truly wretched system. During her lifetime, she had earned the respect of the slaves on her plantation. Often, regrettably, she rejected runaways who pledged loyalty if she purchased them. Since her early childhood years, Hannah put forth great effort in emulating her. Memories of Tressie filled their silence until Miss Hannah spoke.

"Sarah, I forbid you to meet with this shrimper."

"But your father—"

"Do not worry about my father," Hannah retorted. "Sarah, you are not this man's concubine."

"Concubine?" Sarah said, hoping she'd pronounced it correctly. It sounded French and she'd never heard it spoken before.

"Give no more thought to this matter," Miss Hannah said as she stood and ran her hands over her body to smooth her dress. "Until tomorrow ma chérie." She leaned forward, kissed Sarah lightly on her forehead and quickly made her exit.

That night Sarah had a strange dream. She was in the kitchen of the Big House and Miss Hannah entered dressed like the shrimper. She kissed her as the shrimper did.

The next afternoon Miss Hannah arrived thirty minutes late. When she entered the room she anxiously closed the door and put the block of wood that was used to prevent other visitors from entering, into its proper position. She walked to her pupil. Together they looked out the room's only window at the camellia trees.

Sarah watched two indigo buntings take flight from one of

the tree's branches and wondered what had caused her teacher's tardiness, but was not about to ask, when Miss Hannah interrupted their silence.

"You do not have to worry about the shrimper ever again. I spoke with my father and told him this plantation and the entire state of Louisiana will learn what a vile man he is if he continues to arrange such meetings. Mister Dubbonnet is quite respected; however, he would lose this respect if people understood why I have never been asked to marry."

Without looking at Sarah, Miss Hannah went on to explain. "Late one night after an evening of debauchery my father stumbled into my bedroom and forced himself upon me." She recalled her dark room and the smell of fine cognac on her father's breath before going on.

"Prior to that evening, I never laid with a man. I became pregnant. My knowledge of this came a month later when I nearly hemorrhaged to death, rejecting the life of my sibling-child. I was bedridden for months. During this time all kinds of bizarre stories began to circulate. Some said I'd gone mad. The slaves thought God was paying revenge to my father for all of his wrong doings. The stories became so elaborate no man or woman came near me."

Sarah, deeply saddened by her teacher's story, turned to face her and offered the warmest smile she could give before speaking. "I am glad no man came near you—maybe you would have left this place. Then who would have been my teacher?

Miss Hannah, you are the only person who cares for me."

Miss Hannah, moved by her pupil's statement, allowed her tears while looking towards the trees. "My mama used to say there is nothing more beautiful than a camellia tree in April."

Hannah extended her hand to Sarah's face and gently turned her head. She stared intently into Sarah's clear brown eyes. As Sarah returned her teacher's gaze, she experienced a feeling hitherto unknown. Standing so close to Miss Hannah was causing her to grow anxious; about what she did not know. She feared their silence. Could they have possibly shared the same dream?

No poem or Psalm has been written that could accurately recount what followed the end of their gaze.

Miss Hannah placed her arm around Sarah's waist and drew her closer. "Do you know how it feels to kiss someone you love?" she whispered as her eyes searched Sarah's face for a sign to continue.

Sarah closed her eyes, acknowledging for the first time her boundless love for Miss Hannah. In that moment she felt her teacher's soft lips firmly pressed against her own. Her tongue slowly penetrated Sarah's mouth. Their tongues met and slowly embraced.

"Lay with me," Miss Hannah pleaded. Sarah, encouraged by her teacher's tenderness, laid herself out. Miss Hannah knelt on the floor beside Sarah's pallet and began to unlace her pupil's boots. Sarah's heart raced inside her warm chest while

Hannah's dainty hands worked at a speed that would've been greatly appreciated in her father's cotton fields. She freed Sarah of her clothes. Perspiration covered Sarah's welcoming body. Miss Hannah stood and without removing her eyes, unbuttoned the front of her dress.

A rose blush appeared on Hannah's cheeks. She entered the bed and took Sarah into her fervent arms. Both women, patient in their desire, allowed their hands to freely explore. Hannah's fingertips expertly probed and massaged Sarah's exquisite limbs. Sarah never knew of two women who did this to each other. She'd heard many stories from Clara and the other women in the Big House. No story spoke of two women loving each other.

Hannah gently parted Sarah's legs. A sigh of relief escaped her lips when she inhaled her feminine odor. She will insert her fingers like the shrimper does, Sarah thought. It would be acceptable though because her nails were not sharpened or filled with dirt as his were. Miss Hannah did not insert her fingers. What followed was something Sarah had never conceived of. Hannah kissed her on the piece of flesh that tingled when Sarah had touched it during the night. Sarah watched as her teacher lead her into a state of pleasure she had not known before. When she felt herself nearing a great release Sarah closed her eyes. Hannah stopped and began to spread the full length of herself over Sarah. Sarah was amazed at how she covered her—almost completely. Hannah planted kisses over

Sarah's face and neck while rotating her hips above her. Sarah raised her hips slightly and met each of Hannah's movements with a counter movement of her own. The room's air grew thick with their heat. Both women cried out as they melted into each other.

Sarah lay motionless as the feeling subsided—a feeling she had never known before, but would later know repeatedly, gratefully. Miss Hannah held Sarah in her arms until she slept.

Awakened by rumbling thunder outside her room, Sarah greeted her solitude. In place of her lover-friend she found a beautifully pieced quilt. Covered with her gift, she turned her thoughts to the memory of their love.

Remembering Hortense

Lily filled the cast iron kettle once prized by her grandmother with warm water, turned on the stove and sank down in the chair near her kitchen table. She maneuvered slowly and deliberately, then sat quietly with both hands inside the pockets of her green and blue striped housecoat. She watched the light of the moon cast shadows against the wall and waited for the kettle to whistle.

Lily didn't like sounds generally. She found that they derailed her thoughts. A dog's bark carried her mind to imagining the breed of the dog. A crying baby made her wonder about the time of its last feeding. An automobile screeching to a halt caused a detailed scenario of the almost-accident to play itself out inside her head. Thinking that nearly all sounds were disturbances, she resolved to rid herself of everything that made noise. The first of her noise-reduction efforts had been sealing the windows, after which, she set her television and radio outside on the sidewalk.

Lily watched for three days as her thirteen inch RCA black

and white television and Panasonic radio went virtually untouched by her neighbors and passersby. On one afternoon a small boy, who was the fifth or sixth child of her Catholic neighbors across the street, entertained himself by playing with the knobs on the radio and television. Lily found pleasure in watching the child lose himself in some fantastic world of imagination until he was reprimanded by his mother and his playing ceased. On the fourth day the father of the boy crossed the street and rang her bell. The bell didn't sound. Lily had it disconnected some years before. She knew he was at her front door because she'd watched him make his small journey from her kitchen window. She opened the door when she imagined the bell would have sounded.

James, Lily's neighbor, wanted to know if he could take the television and radio home. Lily assured him that that was indeed what she'd hoped someone would do. He politely thanked her, and carried the television and radio away.

Now Lily waited for the kettle to whistle. The kettle whistled every morning promptly at seven when she prepared herself one medium-scrambled egg and two slices of wheat toast to accompany Earl Grey, and occasionally at midnight when an unpleasant dream or eerie sound disrupted her slumber.

The squirrels must have found another way into the attic, she concluded when she was awakened by scratching noises above her head.

The kettle blew, the only noise Lily welcomed. When the kettle sounded, Lily remembered Hortense. She rose from her chair and reached over to remove the kettle from the stove. She half-filled an antique yellow porcelain cup with piping hot water over her tea bag, sank down in her chair and sighed as she wait-ed for the cup to cool. A tear rolled down her cheek as she recalled Hortense's face. Try as she might, Lily Taylor had failed to evict the grief that lived in her heart.

Hortense had been Lily's dearest high school friend. The two grew from awkward adolescent girls into handsome young women. Lily believed the soul-deep love that she had shared with Hortense was the greatest nourishment she'd ever received.

After graduating from high school, Hortense had encour-aged Lily to join her as a summer camp counselor at an elite girl's camp in Vermont. Lily was anxious to earn money to sup-plement the scholarship she'd been awarded to Connecticut Teacher's College. She decided to take the job to put an end to her financial worry and to be close to Hortense, who at the end of the summer was going off to Cornell University to study astronomy.

For as long as Lily remembered Hortense had been fasci-nated by the solar system. During their senior year most of her conversation was about her plans to study with Carl Sagan.

Lily had planned to become a school teacher. The two young women often shared their dreams and career plans. But they never spoke of falling in love. Lily knew this was because they both cherished their love for each other and if left up to her, they would live together in a house far away from Greenwich and everything they knew.

Summer camp days passed too quickly. Lily enjoyed supervising arts and crafts with her fourth and fifth grade group. Hortense met all the challenges inherent in working with preteens with matching enthusiasm and confidence. They'd managed to spend all of their evenings together, sharing their precollege anxieties.

The last night of camp, Lily decided she would give Hortense the bracelet she'd labored over all summer. The bracelet would remind Hortense of all they'd shared and would share in the coming years. With each bead, Lily remembered some fantastic scene from the many days and evenings she'd spent with Hortense Petry. She hoped the bracelet would warm Hortense's heart during the cold Ithaca days.

Lily waited in her cabin. She expected Hortense around ten p.m., after the pre-teen's 'farewell' swimming party. Lily anticipated their night would follow the format of previous nights. They would look at the constellations through the telescope Hortense received from her parents for graduation. Unlike other nights, however, tonight Lily planned to tell her friend how deeply she loved her. The bracelet would accompany the secret—the only secret she'd ever kept from her friend.

A thunderous emergency bell had sounded startling Lily

and disrupting the soliloquy forming in her head. She grabbed her flashlight. Walking towards the cafeteria, where all campers were expected to report if the bell sounded, Lily prayed no child had experienced serious injury.

Once everyone was seated, Joe announced that there had been a terrible accident. The word terrible did not begin to do justice to the event he described, Lily thought. It was horror beyond belief, beyond acceptance. Hortense Petry could not have drowned. Lily sat in disbelief as he relayed the story. Hortense tried to save two novice pre-teen swimmers who'd decided to have their own party in the nearby lake. One of them survived; the boy, Daniel Hawkins. Angel Murray and Hortense Petry did not.

Three days later, after the funeral, Lily had sat on the edge of Hortense's bed in the Petrys' New England home. Mrs. Petry had given Lily the telescope and diary that had belonged to Hortense. Downstairs people offered the Petrys condolences as they filed out of the front door. In the kitchen a tea kettle whistled. Lily read the last entry to Hortense's diary, written the morning of the day she drowned. She wrote longingly of the love she'd always felt for Lily and how she feared the distance that would separate the two once she went off to Cornell. Lily looked at the bracelet she'd made for her friend now dangling from her left wrist. Hortense wrote about the dreams she'd had of sharing a home with Lily and how she hadn't known what to make of those dreams. Lily had clutched the diary to her chest and cried as the tea kettle began to shriek.

At forty-two Lily had not overcome the loss of Hortense. She'd gone through life's motions; graduated from college, started teaching, bought a home, experienced a few relationships. Therapist after therapist tried to assure her that Hortense was not the ultimate love—that she would have to love deeply again if she wanted to have a full life. So, she settled for a life that would not be so full. She settled for a quiet, half-full life.

What her therapists didn't understand Lily shared with her journals throughout the years. What her therapists didn't understand was that she believed in one soulmate. She believed one could find true love very young—in her case at fourteen years of age when Hortense walked into Freshman homeroom. Her love's death didn't change that belief. No. Changing would be unjust to her and her soulmate. She tried to explain this to her few acquaintances—she had no close friends for fear of needing someone the way she needed Hortense.

In her halfness, Lily still found some enjoyment. She identified with the poetry of W.B. Yeats, also a tragic romantic. Knitting kept her hands busy when she was not cleaning house. Raspberry sorbet caused her taste buds to jump start. She didn't know a more pleasant taste but decided Hortense's kiss would have been as sweet. Her fourth grade students introduced her to new worlds and helped her see this world through rose-colored glasses sometimes.

In the first years of her adulthood, her college years, cramming her mind full of Hortense-memories had been easy. She reread both of their journals over and over. After college, she began to imagine her friend's reaction to scenarios from her half-full life. She imagined her friend's advice, her friend's love in a more mature state.

In her halfness, Lily made discoveries about herself. She found that walks through the forest helped her breath easier. Grocery shopping, on the other hand, made her nervous. She never went near a swimming pool or lake. The smell of chlorine nauseated her. She learned to get around town without ever passing a body of water.

Her most recent discovery was her dislike of noises, perhaps because the children at school, not her class but others, were so rowdy. Or maybe it was better for her memories to take shape in silence.

Scratching noises brought Lily back to the present. She made a mental note to phone a roofer first thing in the morning. As she stood, she wiped tears from her eyes. The cup of tea had cooled. She drew several sips from it and retired again.

Breakfast with Dinah

There are many splendid 'first' love experiences—the first glance, the first hand-holding session, the first kiss, the first time you hang up the telephone knowing the woman on the other end has won your heart. The experiences with Dinah are imprinted so indelibly on my mind and heart that I scarcely remember the women who came before her.

The first time I had a clue our relationship would bear such fruit was the morning after we'd made love for the first time.

I like to recall the first breakfast I prepared for us.

Out of nervousness I pull everything out of the refrigerator. Happy that I've found the world's last meat-eating lesbian, I rip open a package of bacon and start to brew my secret blend of coffee—Guatemalan and Ethiopian beans.

Dinah enters the kitchen wearing a fresh shower scent and a rejuvenated air. My nose slightly tickles at the scent of lilacs coming from her short hair.

She smiles, rubs her tummy like a two-year-old, kisses me on the back of the neck, and starts searching the cupboards for coffee mugs. I admire her for making herself at home. She volunteers to help, but I want to prepare this breakfast for her, not with her. I explain this and she resolves to read our horoscopes while I cook. Both of us, Geminis, are promised a four-star day.

I turn bacon, flip French toast, sprinkle cinnamon on it and begin to scramble eggs.

"Um…," Dinah begins. "I love cinnamon baby. I can't believe you're cooking like this. This is so nice. No one, other than my Mam-Maw, has ever cooked this way for me."

Eating has always been one of my favorite pastimes. I conclude that Dinah and I have this in common. She is ravenous. I watch her savor every bit of food that I've placed on her plate. I grow warm watching her eat. My eyes follow her willowy hand as she allows her fork to skate a piece of French toast through syrup speckled with cinnamon.

"You are such a good cook," she says, in the voice she used the night before to thank me for the pleasure I'd given her.

Dinah pauses. She is sitting near the only window in the house that welcomes sunlight's northern exposure. Looking at her, I begin to feel some of the old pain—from being mistreated, misunderstood, and taken for granted—dissolve. I put this image of us onto the canvas of my memory. I am aware now that I had it all wrong. The notion that I'd fall in love in some grandiose vacation spot or in a scene comparable to that of a Hollywood drama was wrong. Nothing could have prepared me for the amount of love I feel during breakfast with Dinah. I place the last bit of food into my mouth. Syrup trickles down my chin.

Dinah uses her napkin to lightly rub it away. I feel cared for. Quietly, we stand and clear the table.

We carry the dishes into the kitchen and place them on the counter. I put my hand on the kitchen faucet and she places her hand over mine. I do not turn on the water. I feel wanted. Dinah carries my hand away from the sink and leads me to the bedroom.

I look out from the bedroom doorway at the table where we've just shared our first breakfast. Our two chairs stand abandoned—away from the table. Somehow I know I will never be able to look back on that room without loving her and loving us. She closes the door. Maintaining my balance is a challenge, for my heart and head greatly anticipate this reunion. I stand near the bed. She walks over to me, kisses me softly.

"I hope you don't have any plans for this afternoon or this evening," she whispers, as we break away from our kiss. I shake my head no.

"Good, because I want to thank you for making such a wonderful breakfast," Dinah sings into the cleft of my chin and neck.

I close my eyes, knowing that she will love me even better than she did the night before, as we lower each other onto the bed.

The Telephone Call

Today I thought about you so long and so hard I knew wherever you were you'd get in touch with me. Today is Christmas and I am alone for another holiday. You are wherever your husband has wisked you and your kids away to this time. Venezuela? Ixtapa? Maybe he wanted snow this year and bought a family ski package in Colorado or Vermont. Foolish man to think that motion will keep you devoted. I've given you plenty of motion, emotion too and it didn't work.

I buy a little cornish hen and fix the trimmings for my meal. I cook the way you would have done. Over my solitary meal I think of my role. My role as the smart, desperate "family friend" who calculates her visits so they coincide with the moment you swish around your adequate-sized kitchen finishing up the preparation of their meal. The last day I saw you, your husband watched a basketball game on the big screen television in the den while in the kitchen I stood behind you—very close as you stirred something on the stove.

"What are you doing?" you hissed at me.

"Too much heat?" I asked you.

You said "yes" in such a manner I knew my presence irritated you. You moved closer to the stove. I wanted you to burn. I backed away, watched you set the table and waited for you to extend an insincere invitation to the dinner you were about to finish. When you asked me to stay I told you it wasn't worth it and left your home angry. I knew you'd call later. The pressure of living a life without magic has always been too much for you. You can't do it without leaning on me. Running to me. Begging me to hold on, to listen, to forgive. I knew you'd call and you did.

Over the phone you sobbed and the begging began. You wanted me to meet you somewhere—"ANYWHERE" because you had to be near me. I have never hated two people more than I hated you and me during that instant. I hated you for believing you have no other choices—for believing in some sick, twisted way that you were being loyal to your family. I hated me for loving you—for having loved you for so long under these circumstances. But I met you. I drove to Jefferson Park, parked by shelter number three and waited. You showed up.

You got out of the car and joined me, giving me a tight squeeze and whispering into my neck how good I felt and how much you needed me. I couldn't afford to repay your tender words. Instead, I asked you a question.

"Where are you supposed to be?"

"I don't know. The kids are in bed. I mumbled something to him on my way out the door. I don't think he heard me."

I grabbed your hand and we went for a walk. We repeated the only conversation we've ever had where you tell me you love me and proceed to list the reasons why you can't leave your husband. When I told you women leave their husbands everyday and get sole custody of the children, you stated the obvious, "I'm not them."

I am done with my meal gulping from my glass of red wine and watching *Terms of Endearment* on public television when the expected telephone ring happens.

"Sorry I haven't called in over a week. Merry Christmas."

"Where are you?" I ask starring at the 5x7 taken of us.

"Palm Springs," you answer wearily. "He and the kids are swimming. What are you doing?" Why in the hell is she telling me about her family?

"Enjoying my holiday," I state in my most sardonic tone.

"Come on Shawn. Let's not do this."

I am alone for yet another holiday. You give your love and blame me for needing it. "You're right Bree. Let's not do this. Let's not do this anymore."

My voice escalates. My heart begins to race. I miss you so much but not nearly enough to equal the amount of hurt and anger I feel. "I'm sitting here feeling lousy, drinking myself into a stupor like I do every fucking holiday because we're not together. I'm not like you Bree. I can't just hop on a plane, go any place, and pretend that I'm not miserable without you. I'm watching *Terms of Endearment* and I know it's just a movie but—what? No, I will not calm down." How dare you even suggest such a thing. Haven't I been patient enough? "I will NOT stop yelling. How can you continue to do this to us?"

You start to cry but I feel nothing.

"Can you even answer my question? How? Why Bree? Why do you continue to hurt me? Us?"

Silence. More silence.

"Bree, I can't play the martyr anymore. It's old. It's real old. God knows I love you. I've loved you for years but I can't go on living like this. No, I'm not giving you an ultimatum. Stop— please. Don't give me 'I love yous.' That's old too. Look, I don't want to do this anymore. I don't want to lie. I don't want to sneak. And I don't want to spend holidays alone—not when I'm feeling this connected to another adult who could bring us together."

You continue to offer apologies, excuses and hysterical "I love yous." Your words no longer have any meaning to me. I realize this as I softly lay the receiver down on the cradle.

I know you won't call back. Not tonight. Not tomorrow. Not on New Year's Eve. I begin to cry wondering how I will get along without you and how it will feel hearing the telephone ring knowing it's not you on the other end. I know this is the beginning of long, hard months of missing you and missing us.

They say the Christmas season is about doing good will to men. I open a second bottle of wine and pour myself a new glass. I toast to the fact that I've done something good. I have participated in the tradition of Christmas-giving by returning the gift of you back to your family. I am free now. Free to enjoy future holidays with a love of my own. Despite the alcohol I consume, I feel the pain of losing you begin to creep in.

Black Triangles, Rainbows and Dykes

The triangle was my absolute favorite shape in kindergarten. When our teacher use to hold up big white signs with colorful shapes on them I would save my breath—my voice—until she held up the white sign with the black triangle on it. When she asked "...And what sign is this?" I would nearly scream, "TRIANGLE!"

I don't know why I developed a fascination for triangles. I guess circles were just too round and squares were just too confining. My love for triangles followed me through elementary school. In junior high I won first place in an art contest. I made a collage out of various ethnically diverse faces I'd cut out of magazines. My collage was shaped like a triangle with a rainbow border surrounding its isosceles edges.

In high school, my family and I found out I was dyslexic, so they put me in this stupid remedial reading and language arts program. I was, however, allowed to continue in the honors geometry. It was really cool being in a class full of juniors and seniors who stumbled into class whenever they wanted, reeking of reefer and sometimes even alcohol.

My senior year of high school I went to an art gallery opening of my mother's best friend. Suzanne, my mom's friend, gave this speech on the importance of promoting contemporary art. Afterwards people started roaming around the gallery, talking to each other in that stupid I'm-a-wanna-be-intellectual way. A huge picture of a solid black triangle on a rainbow surface caught my attention. I walked over to the picture and stared. I was so overwhelmed by the picture and my desire to comprehend its meaning I didn't notice that I was standing very close to a beautiful woman—until she sneezed.

"Bless you," I said. Curious, I asked her, "What do you think this means?"

"It doesn't really mean anything," she began. "It's more like a token of appreciation."

Her tone of voice was so matter-of-fact I decided she must be the artist.

"I love it," I said, extending my hand. "My name is Dorie."

"Thanks. My name is Barbara." She shook my hand firmly.

"You said this painting is a token of appreciation?"

"Yes, to women who were brave enough and proud enough to be truthful about their sexual preferences. In Nazi concentration camps, lesbians were forced to wear upside-down black triangles, and we have kept the symbol alive within the lesbian and gay community. The rainbow is a modern-day symbol of gay pride. Before I started this painting, I read a book about the persecution of gays and lesbians during the Nazi era. I grieved for weeks after reading the book; then I decided to channel my grief into something positive. As a lesbian, I began to feel greatly indebted to the women who paid the ultimate price—just because they were lesbian."

It was getting late and my parents were ready to leave the art gallery. I didn't want to leave because I was enjoying talking to Barbara. She was very intelligent and not at all what I thought a lesbian would be like. My parents had spoken disapprovingly of gays and lesbians whenever footage from some gay march or something was on television. And my mom always escorted me to the beauty salon and to the shopping mall because she didn't want her daughter getting her hair cut "too short" or buying too many pairs of 501s. "After all," she said, "I didn't want to look like 'one of those women.'"

Well, Barbara didn't look like 'one of those women.' Her dark ringlet-hair fell in cascades over her small shoulders, leaving barely an inch-or-so of delicate neck to be seen. Her frame was petite but curvaceous. She wore a pair of corduroys which hugged her hips and firm buttocks and a turtleneck that clung to her bra-less flat chest, advertising nipples that were unmistakably proud of their existence. Everything about Barbara was feminine.

I told Barbara good-bye, and she gave me one of her cards and said if I ever wanted to have coffee and talk, to give her a call.

Later on that night, after I'd had my shower and recalled

Barbara's face a million times, I began to think about the personal bond I'd always had with triangles and if in any way it was related to my subconscious desire to bond with women. I was, after all, the only senior girl who had never been out on a date with a guy—according to my mother. I just wasn't into boys. But I'd never considered the other. I said my prayers and turned out the light. I thought about Barbara some more before I got out of bed to retrieve her card from the back pocket of my Levis. I folded the card until it formed a tiny triangle and I went to sleep with it safely enclosed in my fist.

Meatloaf

Certain times are more difficult than others. My therapist says this is to be expected. But it's been two and a half years since Carmen's passing and I am still grieving her. It's not like our relationship was perfect. It wasn't. She was a liar. She was a bitch. She was a lying, drinking, bitch. A lying, drinking bitch who probably never experienced a sober day during the last three years of our relationship. Still, I stayed. I stayed and I loved her. I loved Carmen even though her lies prevented all real intimacy from ever growing between us. I loved her even though every challenge in her life became just cause for her to seek comfort in a bottle. I loved her—even though moments before she died we argued over the billionth lie I'd caught her in.

"Going to the store to get breadcrumbs for the meatloaf," she yelled at me from the bottom of the stairwell. "If we substitute crackers for breadcrumbs Mama will know the difference. And she won't like it. You know how fussy she is." Her mother was coming over for a sure-to-be strained Sunday dinner.

She came home two hours later with a bent box of breadcrumbs, vodka on her breath and remnants of Samantha's cologne on her clothes. Old Spice-wearing Samantha, the alcoholic who lives around the corner, seduced Carmen on a regular basis.

I confronted her about the cologne. Carmen swore what I smelled was not Sam's Old Spice. But I knew. After minutes of shouting demands for the truth she said "Fuck you. I'm not a two year old. You don't own me." Then she ran out of the kitchen door.

I reached behind the microwave, Carmen's newly designated hiding place, to retrieve her fifth of Ketel One. I poured myself a drink. Then I poured it down the drain and proceeded to empty the bottle the same way. I started to make the meatloaf.

That's about as far as I've been able to get with the story in therapy. I don't remember how the policemen appeared in my kitchen or how their words sounded when they told me Carmen had plowed into the acadia tree at the corner of our block, and killed herself. I don't remember picking up the phone and dialing Carmen's mother, but she didn't come to dinner that evening. I ate the meatloaf alone. After dinner, I buried the empty box of breadcrumbs, the last thing Carmen touched, in the backyard.

The breadcrumb-box funeral marked the beginning of more episodes where I discarded things associated with Carmen.

The day after her death her mother told me she would

make all of the memorial arrangements. I gladly consented. In my mind I could only imagine a memorial service lasting about fifteen seconds in which I would stand and say, "Here lies the lying, drinking bitch I gave my heart to. May she never rest in peace."

I started cleaning our bedroom closet first. I bagged up all of her clothes and shoes. She didn't own a jacket or coat. She believed no one in Los Angeles should buy jackets or coats and always borrowed mine when the weather got chilly. I asked her mother if she wanted any of her daughter's things. She instructed me to give them to Goodwill. After I put several full bags in the garage, where they remain, I started with my clothes. There was the dress she bought for me in Provincetown three summers ago and the scarf she bought me the year we made a special Easter pilgrimage to Rehoboth Beach. God, it was so rainy, so dreary those few days. But we were happy. We stayed in our B&B, read poetry to each other, ate lots of food—take out from the local restaurants—and made love. Carmen had sworn off booz during that period and was acting like the woman who'd swept me off my feet seven years ago. On our last day at the beach she bought me this beautiful indigo scarf because I am notorious for getting sore throats. When I put the scarf up to my nose and inhaled deeply it was still scented by the Delaware rain. Then there was the awful sweater she knitted for me our first Christmas. She decided she was going to stop smoking and took up knitting. After making my sweater she threw away the knitting kit and celebrated by buying a carton of Marlboros. The sweater was so flawed I often wore it just to see the looks of amusement on my colleague's faces. I shoved the dress, scarf, and sweater into a new garbage bag.

I took an empty shoe box and cleared her things off of the dresser. Her loose change, the silver bracelet I'd given her on our last anniversary and her wallet went into the box with one arm swipe. I guess she forgot she'd need money to buy the breadcrumbs. I'm sure once she realized she didn't have it on her Sam gave her the money. Nothing else on the dresser belonged to her. She didn't wear jewelry—making an exception for the silver bracelet. According to her, wearing jewelry would have been denying her butch Latina machisma.

The sheets on our bed smelled a little like her. Not much. I'd recently changed the bedding. If anything, the bed smelled too much like my own scent—a painful reminder of the love we no longer made. During the last year Carmen had been "working late." Drunks put forth no effort in the creativity department. I mean, if I was intentionally feeding someone loads of bullshit at the very least I would spare them the clichés. I'd become accustomed to driving past the bar on my way home from work. Her car was always parked in the same spot—next to Sam's. Sometimes Dicey, the bartender, would phone me and tell me to watch for Carmen because she'd just left the bar. Carmen would go home with Sam and eventually find her way to our home several hours later. The last time Dicey called I told her "Look. You and I both know she's not on her way home. I appreciate your thoughtfulness but please don't call me again." In the midst of my grief I was tempted to phone Sam and ask her if she needed me to come over and change her bed. I'm sure the bereaved home-wrecker's sheets reeked of Carmen.

After ridding our bedroom of Carmen memorabilia I was depleted of all energy. I collapsed on the couch where I ended up sleeping for the night.

The next morning, after realizing it was Easter, I forced myself to go to church. Attending church has always been an important part of my identity—a part of my identity she never understood. Carmen argued that if I'd grown up a closeted Catholic I would have no tolerance for the church either. I schooled her on the fact that Black churches are also extremely homophobic and going to church with folks who referred to gays and lesbians as faggots and bulldykers was hardly affirming. The only difference was, and is, I am not willing to give up my spirituality based on other peoples' issues with my "orientation." I even found a church that was accepting and begged Carmen to go along. She refused. I guess going to a place of serenity, a place where one can reflect and meditate on what is good, paled in comparison to her Sunday afternoon of pool and high-balls.

En route to church I listened to Chanticleer. Their music always relaxes me. My nerves were wrenched. I couldn't believe I didn't have Carmen to worry about anymore. The previous

Sunday on this very route I'd popped in my Chanticleer CD and hoped that Carmen wouldn't overdo it because it would only set a really bad tone for her workweek. Of course to even hope represented wasted energy.

I arrived at church on time but remained in the car an extra fifteen minutes. I knew that if I went in with the crowd, the few people I'd befriended would inquire about her and I couldn't, still can't, say the word 'dead' and Carmen in the same sentence. I concluded that going in late, taking a seat in the back row would save me from seeing or talking to anyone. My plan was successful.

After church I made a salad and took mental inventory of everything in the kitchen that belonged to her. Early in our relationship she often wooed me with gourmet meals. Many of the special utensils and appliances she'd purchased over the years were now covered with dust. I wouldn't work on Sunday but the next day I'd get rid of it all.

Over dinner I remembered the beginning of our end. One tender night Carmen surprised me and pulled up in the driveway right behind me. She hadn't come home directly from work in a long time. We made dinner and drank tea by the fireplace. She asked me to hold her. I remember taking her into my arms believing her way of life had tired her and she was ready to seek professional help. She cried in my arms and explained to me that, "The memories were just too much." She continued insisting I trust that she really loved me and our life together and it was only the memories that made her drink.

Three years ago Carmen's mother lost her only sibling—a brother—to a boating accident. Carmen and I had been together four years, living together three, when it happened. I knew that Carmen was not particularly fond of her uncle Ernesto but I assumed that it was because he represented the heterosexual patriarchal model she so despised. After his funeral she told me and her mother that Ernesto had sexually abused her for years. Carmen's mother went into a tirade. She asked her daughter how she could make up stories and degrade the sweet memory of her uncle Ernesto—who was above all 'a God fearing man.' This and more spoken in hysterical Spanish. I was stunned after four years of loving, laughing, crying, debating, dreaming, fighting, and making-up Carmen failed to tell me something so important. Eventually I managed to calm her and her mother and brought Carmen home. At home she told me everything. I watched carefully and listened patiently. As she talked, I noticed the eyes looking back at me were void of all emotion. Their steel blackness scared me. In that moment I knew we were about to go to war with this demon from her past. Only I hoped that Carmen would fight. I hoped she would allow me to fight with her. She didn't.

Following that evening I suggested we go to counseling. Carmen said she needed to go into therapy alone. I also decided to go into therapy to become a better ally for her. Then she started to dream. First one nightmare a week. Then two, three, and on until it was every night of the week. We were both zombies. Many mornings I'd awake to find her doctoring self-inflicted wounds. During the course of the night she'd scratch herself so deeply she'd be bleeding. She'd apologize for any blood on the sheets and explain "I was fighting Ernesto in my dreams."

Some mornings she could not get herself together enough to go to work. Sometimes I stayed home from work to care for her.

Then the nightmares stopped. She didn't want to talk about Ernesto ever again. She stopped seeing her therapist. We fought and fought over the latter. I didn't mind that we weren't to mention his name but the thought of who Carmen might become without therapy terrified me.

Space is a funny thing. You can't touch it but you certainly feel it when it starts to form a wedge between you and your lover. Carmen stopped wanting to do things with our mutual friends and started frequenting the new bar and spending more time with her new acquaintance—Samantha. I never hung out at the bar. It was my personal boycott against straight proprietors and bankers who encourage gays and lesbians to open bars rather than healthier venues for entertainment. Every year alcoholism statistics increase in lesbian communities as do the openings of new bars. Carmen seemed almost happy that I wasn't into the bar scene.

As she drank she worked less on her career, less around the house, and less on us. She kept long hours and cut off all lines of communication with everybody besides Sam. I knew Sam was a problem when one morning, after I'd awakened in a lonely and desperate state and we had sex, Sam called. Over the phone Sam gave Carmen some sob story about running into her ex at the bar the night before. Luckily, I'd convinced Carmen to stay home the night before to build the entertainment center with me. We missed all the drama that Sam now relayed as "heart breaking," "crushing," "debilitating." When Carmen got off the phone she crawled out of bed and put on her robe. She walked to the kitchen and put on a pot of coffee before coming back to our bedroom to tell me Sam was on her way over because she needed consoling.

In the first place, Carmen was in no fucking place to console anybody. My hurt feelings compelled me to remind her of this. In the second place, we'd just made love. In the third place, was she fucking blind? Could she not see that Sam was trying to come between us and we were already in a very fragile place? Carmen discredited everything I said. So much for the romantic Sunday brunch and walk in the park we'd planned. It was clear that I was waging the war to save Carmen and salvage our relationship on my own. I got up and started getting ready for church. I heard Sam enter the house while I was in the shower. I knew what was to come. I also knew that I was too weak to stop it from happening or to stop myself from getting hurt by it. I wept in the car on the way to church. After church I went home and found a note on the kitchen table:

Gone to lunch with Sam. Misery does love company.

Soon after their lunch date she and Sam started fucking. I knew because Carmen kissed me differently. Obviously, her tongue had forgotten the dance it once did with mine. The new motions she did were faster, rougher, and lacked all sentiment, all love. Greetings once offered in a kiss were reduced to curt "Hellos."

It's easy to recall the things I did after her death. It's impossible for me to talk about my feelings—besides anger. It's almost as if anger is all I'm allowing myself to feel. Dr. Tyler says what's important is for me to be patient with myself and to remain in therapy. I've been seeing her for about seven months now. In the beginning I felt nothing. So, I guess in a way I've graduated. At least I'm experiencing the anger.

There are still days that I feel empty. The emptiness is so great that it's hard for me to remember who I was or how I lived before I knew her. Damn her. How could she not love herself enough to work on her shit. I was willing to go through fire with and for her as many times as necessary. Why didn't she trust that? Why wasn't that enough? Why did she have to fuck around with the booz and Sam? And why the fuck did I stay as long as I did. I guess I thought I could save her. But why did I even want to when she'd become this person that I no longer knew, no longer respected, and no longer wanted to share my life with.

Now I walk around half-alive, half-feeling, half-numb. The

part of me that feels, feels torn, shredded, and on most days, not even salvageable. For so long I thought holding on to Carmen was the hardest thing I'd ever done. Now I know letting go of her is. I miss her so much everyday I wonder if I run myself into a tree maybe I'll wind up in the same place she is. And maybe in this place there will be no sexual abuse, no abuse of any kind, no alcohol and no space for scavenger dykes who prey on the weaknesses of relationships. Maybe in this place there will be just room enough for two women to love each other; to give to each other; to gladly take from each other. I wonder about this place. Does it exist? Is Carmen there? Is she waiting for me? In her transition to that place did she turn back into the woman I met seven years ago on the steps of a flower shop, banging on the door, begging the clerk not to close just yet because we both needed flowers for Mother's Day. She was so full of life then and so mine. I knew right away.

Sometimes I have dreams about this place. She is the Carmen who made all the happy, silly clichés about love come true for me. She made me consider the notion of 'forever' when she smiled. In my dreams we are alone in this place, utterly vulnerable and equally trusting. We feel healthy and whole and we are happy. A state we never enjoyed but something I always envisioned with her.

During our last session I told my therapist I never stopped believing—that's why I stayed. I believed we could be happy. Now through all of this grief I'm learning what it means to love wisely. To love wisely means to love someone who also believes. I tell myself that the woman who believes is out there and as I work on healing I'm waiting for her.

New Kid On The Block

I was "out," formally that is, one month when Gypsy's opened. My older lesbian friends who'd taken me under their wings and exposed me to night life in clubs that catered to the older, more sophisticated lesbian, felt sorry for me because they knew I was uncomfortable being hit on by women my mother's age and sometimes even my grandmother's age. My younger friends asked why I even went out with the older women if I knew what the outcome would be. They didn't understand it was important for me to be in that setting. Being gay is more than an attribute like having green eyes or hairy legs; it's a lifestyle. Sometimes I feel as if my "straight" friends will never understand that. Besides, I liked the club scene. Nothing floats my boat more than doing a provocative dance move with a woman.

One Sunday afternoon I was having lunch with Margie and her partner Pat when they told me they'd heard about a new club opening. They sensed my disinterest and went on to tell me, "It's for baby-dykes." I immediately became enthused. You have to understand when a woman is newly "out" she's eager to get involved with someone. I had so much love to give and couldn't wait to find the lucky recipient.

The following Saturday, I invited Jamie, a bisexual friend of mine, to come along with me to check-out Gypsy's. I wore a denim bra, a mini-denim skirt, thigh-high cable knit socks, my favorite pair of worn leather boots, and of course my labrys necklace. I was a walking definition of lesbian chic if I must say so myself.

Gypsy's turned out to be a real hole in the wall. The dance floor was slanted and over-waxed, thus making it damn near impossible to slow dance without colliding into another couple. But I danced anyway. In fact, I danced all night long. The bar stools were very uncomfortable but the bartender, Cindy, was a real cutie and knew how to make an excellent Bloody Mary. I drank more than a few. The women were young and good-looking so, despite the club's dilapidated condition, illogical dance floor and uncomfortable bar stools I knew I'd found my new spot.

That night I met Rebecca. Rebecca was exactly the kind of woman I'd envisioned myself with. Shorter than me by a considerable amount with short, curly red hair, she had a broad and flat chest, lovely rounded hips and big legs. Rebee, her preferred nick-name, had this tomboyish flare going for her but there was something very sapphic about her.

We exchanged numbers before Jamie and I left the club. Sunday night Rebee called and I invited her over. I lied and told her I was really in the mood for a good game of Monopoly and would love her company. Monopoly! Yeah, I know, corny. I couldn't tell her the truth, that in the twenty-four hours I'd known her I'd masturbated twice—with her in mind.

When Rebee arrived wearing a sky blue sun dress with spaghetti straps, exposing her beautiful shoulders generously speckled with raspberry-tinted freckles I thought I'd die.

We played Backgammon instead of Monopoly, and after Rebee beat me for the third time I suggested we do something else. We moved from the kitchen table to the floor, where we looked through my old scrap books and talked about our child-hoods. Isn't it crazy how you try to legitimatize the fact that you want to fuck a perfect stranger by trying to learn everything about her past in a few minutes? I told her I was an English major and she told me she'd been a Psych major before she dropped out of college to become a waitress. She said her back was tired, so we moved to the sofa.

I asked Rebee if I could count the freckles on her face. She didn't have many. There we were face to face—me counting and Rebee staring into my eyes. "Eleven" I said. Rebee kissed me. Her tongue darted into my mouth so quickly it took me a few seconds to understand what was happening. When I realized I was inside her sweet mouth, my tongue began to chase hers and they entwined themselves so naturally it was almost as if it had been rehearsed. While kissing her, I began to push the sides of her dress upward, which much to my surprise was already conveniently gathered around her waist. I put my hand between her warm thighs and began to rub her satin crotch. With one swift motion, my finger was inside her and she let out an earthy moan.

Ending the kiss so we could both catch our breath, I led her to the floor and told her I wanted to taste her. Rebee quickly removed her damp panties and supporting herself on her knees positioned herself perfectly over my face. I took one look at her fiery-red bush and my tongue dived between her lips in search of her pearl.

Rebee put her hand between my legs and rubbed ferociously. I felt my clit stiffen and thought it would bust the seam of my cotton shorts. Rebee began to rock back and forth. She smelled delicious. As my tongue alternated between soft strokes and harder ones, her rocking turned into wild bucking. Within seconds I felt her sweet juices trickle down on to my mouth and chin. Like a pussy cat savagely lapping every drop of her cream, I came too. She kissed my face and collapsed on the floor next to me.

"That was grrrrreat," she said imitating Tony the Tiger.

"Um hum," I agreed wiping my mouth with the back of my hand. I then turned over on my side and leaned over her face to kiss her. Her taste lingered in my mouth long after she'd gone home.

Four orgasms later Rebee moved in. I loved having her as a roommate, a fuckmate, but more importantly she was becoming my best friend. Our living arrangement was perfect. Rebee, a domestic Goddess, spoiled me by having lunch or dinner ready for me everyday after class. She was a good cook, she was funny, and she held me real tight when I came, I liked that. We even came together lots of times—something Margie and Pat said was virtually impossible.

Then one night after my psychology class I ran home to show Rebee the test I'd aced, which of course she'd helped me study for. When I opened the apartment door, I called her name and didn't get a response, nor did I smell food. I began to panic. Rebee had requested she only be scheduled for breakfast shifts at the restaurant so we could spend our nights together. It suddenly occurred to me that it was the first time in three months that Rebee wasn't waiting for me.

I called Carmichael's and some chick told me Rebee'd left "hours ago." I figured as much. I sat at the kitchen table what seemed like an eternity, doodling on the newspaper. The phone rang; I answered it. It was Miss Somebody. I didn't know a Miss Somebody. She was calling from St. Mark's Hospital. Rebee had had an epileptic seizure in the grocery store and it was grand mal. What? Seizures? Grand mal?

I slammed down the phone and ran to the table near the door to grab the keys. Damn. Rebee used the car during the day. Damnit, I'll run. I thought, and I did. I ran thirteen blocks.

When I reached the hospital information desk they wanted to admit me because I was so out-of-breath and I guess I looked pretty flushed.

When I entered Rebee's room the sight of her reminded me of a rag doll I had when I was growing up. She looked pale and weak. She looked like someone I didn't know. The nurse grabbed my arm and said, "This hit her pretty hard," as if I knew her seizure history and should make note of it. She explained she'd given Rebee a mild sedative before she left us alone.

"Why didn't you tell me?" I said as I sat down on the edge of her bed.

"I thought you'd break up with me. Who wants a handicapped girlfriend?"

"What a dumb thing to say. I want you Rebecca, you know that. I love you and I don't care what happens now or in the future, nothing will change that."

Rebee grabbed my hand and squeezed it tight while I looked out the window. I laughed and she said, "What? What's so funny?"

"I was just thinking what if you'd had a seizure while I was going down on you? I'd have to call the paramedics. Shit, would that be embarrassing to explain?"

I was trying to make light of the situation or hide the fact that I was terribly afraid. In just a few months Rebee had become the center of my universe and to think I could have lost her. I blinked twice to prevent the tears from falling. My effort was in vain. I turned to face Rebee and noticed tears stood in her huge green eyes.

"I'm glad I have you," she whispered.

"Yeah, me too," I said. "I love you. And is there anything else I should know about you Miss O'Donnell?"

She gave me that silly, mischievous grin I'd come to adore.

"Yeah, I'm Irish."

It Happened One Sunday Afternoon:
A True Story

Most fifteen year old girls experience a major crush on one of two types of adolescent males. There is the scrawny, lanky guy who really isn't cute or outgoing but he's sweet and knows how to make the awkward and vulnerable pubescent female feel special. Then there is the "macho" jock, who is cute and even has a little hair on his face to prove the presence of testosterone. I was different. I met Vita, which isn't her real name, when I was fifteen. We met at church. I was sitting on the pew, beside my grandmother when Vita, who was several pews before us, turned around to see who was in the congregation. Our eyes met and no one before or since has ever given me a smile that said so much.

That evening over supper I casually asked my grandmother who that woman was. I described her as best as I could. That wasn't very difficult since I'd memorized her face in a matter of seconds. It didn't take my grandmother anytime to name that woman. She went on to tell me about Vita Rose (I chose that pseudonym because Vita means life, and roses were my love's favorite flowers. Every time I see a rose I am reminded of her life and how much she shaped mine). Vita had been an elementary school teacher and registered nurse. She'd been married to a photographer who had been well-known in the community. They'd had two beautiful children, etc. Grandmother told me that day had been the first Sunday Vita had been to church in quite some time. She'd just lost her husband and had been grieving for months.

The next Sunday, following the benediction, I approached Mrs. Rose. I was a little nervous but I wanted her to know me. The moments before I introduced myself still seem suspended in time. I told her who I was, I mentioned who my grandmother was since I'd learned the previous Sunday they had belonged to the same Women's Bible Class for over twenty-five years. She was very cordial and told me to look her up in the phone book and give her a call.

That evening I wrote Mrs. Rose a long letter filling her in on the previous fifteen years of my life. I wrote the whole evening long and mailed it the following morning. A couple days passed and one evening my grandmother's telephone rang. I knew the instant it rang it was Mrs. Rose. My grandmother called me to the phone quite elated that such a nice woman—"educated too"—had taken an interest in me. On the telephone Mrs. Rose complimented my letter-writing style and told me she was very "impressed" with me. I explained to her that I was only visiting my grandmother and would be returning to my home state of Illinois at the end of the summer. We made plans to keep in touch.

Over the next two years I wrote hundreds of letters and we both made AT&T richer! Vita was understanding, easy to talk to, and always cheerful. She was constantly encouraging me and insisting I build big dreams. Her optimism was contagious. Vita listened well. She knew how to offer her advice without sounding harshly critical of my plans or ideas. I found myself sharing every aspect of my life with her and looking forward to visits with my grandmother more than ever. I look back on those years now and realize that was the onset of my first lesbian relationship. The essence of a lesbian relationship is the spiritual and emotional connecting of two females, which can be celebrated through lovemaking and continuous nurturing of one another. I connected with Vita, despite the fifty years age difference.

During this time I was messing around with high school boys because it was the 'normal' thing to do but in the back of my mind thoughts of holding and kissing Vita were causing me to question my sexuality.

That was the spring my mother decided we'd surprise my grandmother for the "Mother's Day" holiday. I decided I would share my feelings with Vita. Of course I was deathly fearful yet there was no way around it. She had to know that thoughts of loving her had been occupying my mind. That Sunday afternoon after church I went home with Mrs. Rose. I will never forget the anxiety I felt. A small part of me feared rejection. In fact, it crossed my mind that I could lose the friendship I'd grown to cherish above all else. A greater part of me however, sensed Vita harbored some of the same emotions.

I pray that the following memory never escapes me and so by writing this I know our love is somewhat immortalized.

After we were inside her house Mrs. Rose asked me to unzip the back of her dress—she wanted to change into a housecoat. While unzipping her dress I held my breath. As I gently tugged on the zipper, which as luck would have it was difficult to manipulate, her bare skin became visible. Immediately, I felt a confusing mixture of desire, fear and anxiety.

She hung up her dress and sashayed around the room while I sat on the edge of the bed utterly stunned at how beautiful her body was. When Vita asked me why I was so quiet I told her I had something very important to say. She sat down on the bed beside me, took my hand in her own and began to gently rub my back with her free hand. In this position she lovingly coaxed the words out of me. In an almost inaudible voice, with my head down, I whispered, "I'm in love with you and I want to make love with you." Vita was quiet for several seconds—which seemed like an eternity—then she casually said, "I feel the same way."

We spent the rest of the afternoon talking about the extraordinary age difference, how people would react, how she could never "come out" and how we had both arrived at the state we were in. We decided to be very careful so no one in her family or in her circle of friends would find out and I falsely swore I would not share our affair with any of my friends.

I didn't exactly know how to make love to a woman but on that afternoon nothing was more important to me than pleasing Vita. I wanted to know every inch of her and I wanted to know how it felt to experience lovemaking with someone who you know loves you. I hadn't considered what Vita could do for me, my thoughts were completely filled with how I could rejuvenate a love-starved soul. Overwhelmed by the fact that she was crossing the line of physical intimacy—with a woman—Vita was actually too nervous to let any lovemaking take place. At least she was on that particular Sunday afternoon. We spent the remainder of the evening holding each other. This picture remains clear in my memory—Vita in her white lace slip and thigh-high panty hose and me still in my church dress. Before I left Vita gave me a kiss—a long exploratory kiss—a promise kiss—a kiss that said "there will be more, just be patient." A kiss unlike any I'd ever experienced with a male.

That was the Sunday afternoon I came out to myself. It felt exhilarating. I knew in time I would have to share it with friends and I did. Of course, I got the expected, "She's too old," and "You need counseling." It didn't bother me though because for the first time I felt loved and if I was a freak or she was a freak...then in my opinion we were just two freaks in love. But how lucky I considered myself for experiencing something so wonderful with someone so wonderful.

Vita and I spent two years together. It is an indescribable feeling when two souls collide in the safety of knowing their lover is filled with only the utmost care and kindness. I experienced this type of collision with Vita. She has since passed away and mere words cannot accurately account for the void I feel within my heart. I know our love was strong because I feel her love from the grave. I hear her whispers of encouragement in the night winds. On really difficult days I can feel her embrace and even smell her fragrance—White Shoulders. I regret we weren't able to display our love in the presence of others, I regret we had to go to so many measures to keep her family and friends ignorant about what was really going on. Although, when I look back I think some of them must have had an idea—you can't really disguise true love. I do not and will not ever regret "us" or the fact that I discovered me, and I discovered love and it all happened on one Sunday afternoon.

Tennessee

"I have reservations under the name Brown. Lynn Brown."

Anxiously eyeing the desk clerk I say my fifth silent prayer
for Nora's safe arrival into Nashville. The attendant's eyebrows
furrow in a look of puzzlement and I remember that I have
requested one room with a single King-sized bed for Nora and
me. Without saying a word, he nervously opens a drawer
beneath the computer and takes out two plastic-card room
keys. I accept them. Before I turn to leave the desk he mumbles
something.

"Uh, Ms. Brown. You have a message."

Oh no. Shit.

"She's missed her flight," I say in an embarrassingly whiney
voice. Nora often says I expect the worst from her. I immediately imagine the scenarios surrounding Nora's missed flight.
She's overslept. Or she said an extended farewell to her cats.
The attendant hands me a small piece of green paper. I dis-
dainfully accept it. The date and time are neatly written along
with the message: Nora Blair called. Flight delayed. Blizzard in

Kansas City. Will call as soon as she knows something. I fold the paper and shove it into my purse. Bending to pick up my travel bags, I tell myself there is no need to hurry. Nora and I will not be making love this afternoon and she will probably miss my presentation.

The sixth annual 'Women In Power Conference' brought me out of my home city, New York, to the middle of Tennessee in the dead of winter. Being a graduate student was proving to be the most challenging task I'd ever committed myself to. The hardest part of graduate study being the distance from Nora, who made her home in the Republican land of Oz. I grudgingly make my way to room 412.

In three hours I would present a paper on 'romantic friendships' in the literature of nineteenth-century American women writers. Nora's absence would mean I'd have to call on my subjects as muses. I'd found my research on the writings of Sarah Orne Jewett, Mary Wilkins Freeman, and Constance Fenimore Woolson affirming. I hoped to prove to the panel, and my audience, that the act of writing about same-sex desire between women is not a twentieth-century phenomenon.

"Oh well," I think aloud as I unpack a bottle of shiraz, bottle opener, two glasses and candles. "I've hauled my romancing tools in vain."

After unpacking I decide to take a hot shower. Maybe if I don't concentrate on Nora's absence she might miraculously appear. I try not thinking about her but as I run my hands down the slopes of my sudsy breasts, my nipples respond with a shrill tingling reminding me of just how much I need her.

I put on my latest investment from Victoria's Secret, a lacy new bra and panties, that I'd hoped to model for Nora. Just as I resolve to surf the cable channels, a knock lands on the door.

"Who is it?" I ask.

"It's me," I hear Nora answer in an excited tone tainted with a smidgen of exhaustion. Upon opening the door I decide some clichés are worth repeating because truly she is a sight for sore eyes. She looks lean and sexy in a tight-fitting sweater, a pair of Levis and black leather boots. Her hair has been cut recently and she smells divine.

In the doorway we grab each other and hug tightly. Nora lovingly and teasingly scolds me for coming to the door nearly naked. I know she approves by the sex gleam in her eyes. Closing the door behind her, she gently pushes me onto the bed. The first kiss, after being apart since Christmas vacation, charges my body with a heat so intense I know it will be diffi-cult to wait until after the presentation. With any luck, I won't have to. Our mouths hold a reunion while our hands become re-acquainted with each other's bodies. I back Nora onto the bed. Lying on top of her, I begin to grind in a slow rotating motion. Her jeans are stimulating both of us. I feel myself get-ting moist as Nora's breathing becomes rapid. She cradles my face with her hands and gently pulls our mouths apart. Staring into my eyes she says, "We don't have time baby. You have to get ready to present your paper."

I can't wait, my eyes reply.

"Right after you're finished I'll make love to you," Nora promises.

Remembering she never breaks a promise I give her a 'til then' kiss and slowly lift myself off of her.

I am calm as I listen to a Connecticut professor deliver a paper on the love letters of Virginia Woolf and Vita Sackville West.

In class I usually worry up to the last minute about my word choice, content, or the rate at which I speak. I attribute my calm to the fact that Nora and I are making eye contact. I wonder if she is formulating a master plan to seduce me. Whatever she is going to do, it won't take much. I allow my eyes to travel all over her body as I hear the loving pet names Virginia used when addressing Vita. I start at her legs, crossed at the ankles, and my eyes linger at her imagined-nude thighs spreading for me. My eyes continue their fantasy voyage, resting on her soft triangular mass of curly hair. I moistened my lips with my tongue and Nora blinks her eyes double time and cracks a smile. She's reading my mind. I hear my name announced and realize it is time for my presentation. I glance back at Nora as she mouths 'good luck' to me. I stand, smooth out my dress and take my place before the podium. I feel confident.

During the question and answer session members of the audience compliment my delivery and after the panel several more people extend positive remarks on the content of the paper. Nora affirms that I have given a terrific presentation before asking me to help her find a restroom. After she declines the first few restrooms we come to, I begin to get irritated. I desperately want to catch the shuttle back to the hotel and reap the benefits of her promise. Nora explains that she wants to be in an area with the least amount of conference-attendee traffic. Finally, we find a secluded restroom on one of the floors where classrooms aren't being utilized for panel space.

Inside the bathroom Nora leads me into the last stall. After closing the door she hangs both of our purses on the hook and takes me into her arms.

"I am so proud of you," she begins. "You are going to make a fine professor one day."

I welcome her kiss. She backs me into the corner of the stall and starts roaming my body with impatient hands. I feel the moisture between my legs increase when she cups my breasts and encircles my ear with her tongue. I open my mouth to let out a moan and she covers my lips with her own, sucking in my tongue in one swift motion. With one hand holding the back of my neck she places her other hand under my dress and begins to gently massage my mound. I tug on her tongue lightly with my teeth. She stops kissing me to asks, "Do you want me inside of you?" I love that she never takes anything for granted. Between quick breaths I manage to utter a "yes—pleassseee." She inserts her middle finger deep inside my sex and proceeds to tell me how wet I am and how much she loves and needs me until I come.

We are straightening our clothes and exiting the stall when two women enter the bathroom. We giggle. We are sharing the same thought—that could not have been timed more perfectly.

As we wash our hands, Nora inquires about what is next on our itinerary. There are lots of wonderful panels going on: women and economics, women and health issues, women and crime, women and almost everything under the sun, but I only have one plan for the remainder of the evening.

"Let's go back to our room," I suggest. Nora smiles sheepishly as she tosses the paper towel into the trash and opens the door for me.

Losing Sight of Lavender

Numb. I'm sitting in a group session. Our leader just asked us to write down the word that best captures how we felt when we learned we have the HIV virus. I can think of no other word besides numb. My English degree from Princeton affords me no greater, more accurate word. Annie, our leader, collects seven cards from those of us who form the crescent shaped circle. I wonder about my T-cell count.

A couple of months ago when I first started coming to these group meetings, I didn't find writing words or thoughts on index cards very therapeutic or helpful in any way. I keep coming back because I figure at least I'm labeling my feelings—at least I'm feeling, which is something I've been afraid to do ever since I found out.

Sometimes I write mean, hateful, even obscene words on the cards. Despite what anybody prints on these cards we are all scared shitless, mad as hell at the world, and we wonder what death will feel like. Sometimes I think these index cards, Annie and this west-side community center don't alter my fate so why do I bother? Then I remind myself that it is all I have now—that's why I bother. When I step into this place, I feel like I am buying myself a little more time. I am encouraged to feel here. Outside I am constantly worried about the time. Time to rest. Time to eat. Time to take medicine. Time to take more medicine. There is no time to feel.

Here, in the presence of my group, I feel it's my time to be human. This session is almost over. I know this by Annie's somber expression.

It's five o'clock. I know by the signals my watch gives me. My watch beeps twice and then vibrates against my wrist. The vibration reminds me to take the crixivan one hour before each meal. I wave good-bye to Annie, the others, and head down the hall to the water fountain. Having forgotten my water bottle this morning forces me to drink from the fountain. My doctor would label this 'risky behavior.' I place the pill on my tongue, lower my head, and allow my lips to meet the spouting water. The water's coolness awakens my lips and the rest of me. I swallow. Go down baby. I hope this shit works. Another draw from the fountain. I think about protease inhibitors, decreasing viral loads, my right to live.

It's raining outside. Gray skies close in on me. I inhale deeply. I hate rainy weather—makes me feel like I'm suffocating or on my way to a funeral. I hate this sky—full of clouds threatening to explode at any moment. I wish for blue skies accompanied by the sun.

I see a young woman ahead of me. She tilts her head backwards and opens her mouth to taste the rain. I envy her for welcoming the rain. She is not afraid of death; I can tell this by the light in her eyes. She brings her head up to its normal position and flashes me a Kodak smile. Perfect. Too perfect. No. She is certainly not afraid of death. I turn the corner, collide with the voices of my mother and doctor.

"Sael fight this. You must fight this every step of the way."—Mom.

"Fighting this disease entails nutrition and exercise."—doctor.

I open a door, step into a small over-crowded market, begin my search for the perfect tomato, perfect avocado, perfect head of lettuce.

The subway appears to bulge at its seams. Dirty, noisy, packed full of people. I step in. The doors close behind me. This is not a joy ride. Mouths spouting foreign languages meet my ears like some wicked cadence. Laughing faces contort themselves in my mind. They become weeping clowns with abnormally large crimson tear stains on their alabaster faces. This is not a joy ride, but I make it to my stop anyway.

Nothing but bills. Slam mailbox shut. Unlock the door, flip on light switch. Toss envelopes on the table, give the studio a once over. Answering machine light blinking. For once I wish it was a woman other than my mother. Push "play."

"Hi Sael. It's Mom. It's storming here so I'll be brief. Your brother got into Penn. That was his top choice. Just thought you'd want to know. You should call and congratulate him. Sael, I hope you are thinking about our last conversation. Why don't you move back home? Philadelphia is not as cosmopolitan as your New York but it's dreadfully dirty and dangerous in that city. I worry about you. I'd feel more comfortable with you here—at least I could take care of you. Oh shoot. That was thunder—better go. Love you. Hope you're feeling well." Long beep. "End of messages."

Salad for dinner. More medicine for dessert. My tears for a nightcap. I'm reminded of Harlem Renaissance poet Georgia Douglas Johnson, who once wrote 'I want to save all the tears I weep and sail to some unknown place.' I reach under my futon for my black notebook and allow my fingers to sail across the pages. I write until the pen slips from my hand.

"Ms. Ross your test came back positive."

My doctor pauses. Silence reinforces my reality. I despise this room, this moment and my illness. I despise every transfusion—efforts to prolong my life actually sentencing me to a long death. I worry about Jocelyn and Marta—the only lovers I've had. My memories of love transform into feelings of fear, shame, guilt.

I remember I am not in this silence alone. I make eye contact with Dr. Sawyers. She's mouthing words I can't hear. I am numb. I hear nothing—at least for awhile. Then a word becomes audible. Asymptomatic. Dr. Sawyers is explaining to me that I am asymptomatic.

"Sael you are in what we refer to as the asymptomatic stage. The average time span of this stage is variable, but usually most people show no signs of HIV infection for five to six years. That time span can be extended by taking antiretroviral drugs such as AZT, crixivan, and proper nutrition and exercise."

"And then what?" I ask. I've seen pictures, I've seen enough movies to know where this road ends. "What happens after the asymptomatic stage?"

"Well, when the cd4 cell count or t-cell count falls between five-hundred and two-hundred most people begin to develop HIV symptoms. This is what is referred to as the symptomatic stage. Our goal is to prevent your t-cell count from dropping. We'll do this by putting you on antiretroviral medicines as soon as possible."

My time is running out.

Eyelids flutter open. Halogen light causes me to squint. Night shirt stuck to my chest. Awakening in this state night after night. Beep. My watch gives my wrist a slight jolt. Time for the d4t-stavudine and the ddc-dideoxycytidine. Gotta take both of them to combat what AZT could do alone. AZT, the prescriptive messiah for most but not for me—causes anemia. Low red-blood cell count warrant transfusions.

Throw sheets back, walk to kitchen. Swallow the .75 milligrams of d4t and ddc. Hands begin to numb. Feet begin to tingle. Peripheral neuropathy is a small price to pay for extended life. Feet begin to burn. This must be how it feels to walk on hot coals or through the Mojave desert barefoot. I'll never do those things, I remind myself as I attempt to fall asleep. What a trade off.

Dreaming this time of Tabu Shatzu, my favorite Japanese restaurant on the upper East side. No more sushi. The equation is simple—raw food equals lowering immune system equals death. Dreaming of sushi. My tongue is asleep but I am tasting mild tuna, salty salmon, inari and tekka makki rolls. Never again or only in my dreams. Next time I dream this dream I will invite a beautiful woman to dine with me.

I am always surprised when morning arrives. Glance at clock. Another day I will be late to the museum. Sitting on the edge of my bed I imagine Rembrandt's Bathsheba painted in 1654. I am posed like she is.

Walking to the museum I console myself with the knowledge that each step I take brings me closer to immortality—the immortality of art. Before heading to the cafeteria, where I work, I search for Bathsheba. In her somber face, the melancholy tilt of her head and the dejected posture of her tired body I see a perfect reflection of my emotions. Thank you Rembrandt for understanding. Now I can work.

Museum is slow this morning. Usually more high school kids and NYU art students. There is a beautiful woman walking towards me. She buys a cup of coffee. I try to direct her to the sugar and the creamers—dairy and non. She tells me she likes it black. Me too. I wonder how much we have in common and then remind myself why that doesn't matter.

The afternoon passes more slowly than the morning. I look forward to group session.

Tonight Annie tells us to remember something positive about our childhood. I remember lots of things but I don't know if they are positive. I remember my mother and father defining leukemia to the carefree but-always-tired child I was. I remember hospital visits, blood transfusions. I remember pain and fear, loneliness and feeling forever on the verge of death. I remember the nine year old girl who died in the bed next to mine at Johns Hopkins hospital when I was recuperating from my third transfusion—age ten. I remember her lavender gown and the lavender sheets on her special bed. I was jealous of her lavender gown because I wore the plain, thin hospital gown. Looking back, I laugh at that feeling. What I wouldn't give now to feel anything other than fear and isolation. I remember asking my mother the name of the little girl when they told me she died. She told me her name was Jonquil. That Christmas I named my doll after her and made her a lavender dress.

Jonquil in lavender became my symbol of hope. Each time

I got sick I promised my doll I would get better so I could continue to be her mommie. I carried her everywhere and was always aware of my promise.

I hear Annie in the background instructing us to write down our favorite thing from childhood. I begin to feel while I continue to remember. Forever I have felt on the verge of death. Somewhere along the journey between childhood and adulthood I lost sight of hope. I lost sight of lavender. Tears moisten my cheeks and my heart flutters at the prospect of feeling other than numb. I scribble lavender on the card and begin to feel like I'm on the verge of hoping. Hoping for the moment, hoping for tomorrow, hoping for life.

Bitter Wine

Seems like every time I decide to do right the devil just takes a hold of my soul and makes me do wrong. Some folk don't believe in the devil but he ain't made up, that's for sure! Sure as there is a God, there is a devil. The devil showed up on my doorstep this morning. Well, it wasn't no serpent or Booga-Man dressed in red. No, but sometimes the devil will tempt you with a pretty package.

I woke up this morning excited about seeing an old friend of mine. Priscilla Ann Walker-Davis was my best girlhood friend. She moved away right after high school. Said our small town was no place for a girl like her. I agreed. After she left I went on with my intentions to marry Lee. You know, sometimes intentions ain't got nothing to do with desires.

You couldn't find anybody in Tyler half as good looking as Priscilla. Even as a child she looked womanly. She had shapely legs and a behind the fellas just couldn't help patting unless Priscilla fought 'em—which she did on occasion. She had a certain way she could look at you—if she liked you. She did something special with her eyes. Seem like she could make 'em light up. I used to watch her talk to other people but I didn't see it in her eyes then. No, I only saw her eyes dazzle when she looked at me .

Priscilla was always special in class cuz she had two last names. Her mama married twice and each time she married she made Priscilla carry the new name. When we was in fourth grade Lottie, another one of my friends, told Priscilla she had a name like an old woman. She also told her she better not be like her mama and marry two different men or she would have the longest name in the world. Priscilla said she didn't intend on marrying.

Yeah, that child know she was pretty. Her skin was like red-clay with just a dab of brown and she had a beautiful complexion. Her hair was soft and wavy. 'Fact, I envied her for not having to use the hot comb. I imagine she could've won a beauty contest if she'd kept those scissors out of her head. I remember when we was seven years old. Priscilla used her art scissors to cut her hair. Since we was best friends I told her I would cut my hair off too, even though I knew my mama would skin me alive if I came home without my braids. Priscilla told me she didn't want me cutting my hair.

And tough. That girl know she was tough cuz every time she cut her hair her mama would beat her. The beatings didn't stop her. She seemed proud when she showed me where the switch had cut the skin right above her behind and left a scar.

Sometimes during recess I'd ask Priscilla if I could see that scar. We'd go behind a tree and she'd unfasten her pants, cuz she never wore a skirt, and hold them open in the back so I could look inside. She never got tired of me asking and I never got tired of asking. Must've seen that scar a thousand times before graduating from the eighth grade.

By the beginning of high school Priscilla was wearing her hair cut close like a man's. I always liked it that way.

Even though all the girls looked up to her, mainly cuz they had to because she was so tall, Priscilla only talked to me. I asked her once why she didn't hang with the other girls and she said "I can live without 'em." Made me feel kinda special, like she couldn't live without me.

My mama said it was something strange about Priscilla only having one friend. Sometimes Mama would even lie and tell her I wasn't home when she came by the house for me. I never asked Mama why she lied cuz Daddy said on account of me being her only child, Mama was just being selfish. I believed that for some time, but one night when I was sitting on the steps eavesdropping—I did this to hear the church gossip every thursday evening when Mama came home from choir rehearsal—I heard Mama tell Daddy, Priscilla Ann was an odd child always cutting her hair and she didn't want me socializing with such a mannish girl.

Seem like the older we got, the closer we got, the less people understood Priscilla. In high school the boys didn't bother

her anymore. But they started bothering me—at least Lee Watson did and I fell in love with him for it. I loved Priscilla but I didn't want people to think I was odd too. It didn't bother her when we walked downtown and people would say, "Hi Leta, how are your folks?" And ignore her. That kinda thing would've just crushed me.

By the beginning of our senior year Priscilla decided to move to New York and study acting. She was pretty enough to be an actress and tough enough to make it in New York City. During this time Lee Watson and I was doing some serious courting. By Easter time he proposed and I accepted. We married right after graduation.

I went to secretarial school for a little while but had to drop out on account of Lee and I were fixin' to have a baby. After Lee jr. came Alice and then Imogene. Between the babies came letters from Priscilla filled with exciting stories about life in the Big Apple. She became an actress, even directed a few plays and was in the company of big time folk. She wrote me every time she attended some fancy party where she'd been in the company of the mayor, some famous jazz singer or a sculptor. She always wrote that none of those folks were as special as me. I didn't believe her but it was still nice to read.

I hadn't seen Priscilla in thirty-six years when my bell rang this morning. She'd been in France on vacation when Lee passed away last month. She came running to Tyler soon as she heard the news.

When I saw her standing on my porch all duded up in a fancy black pants suit and expensive shoes, smiling at me with those sweet brown eyes that always looked at me like I was special—a look Lee never mastered—a feeling of anger overcame me. Now I knew that was nothing but the devil himself making me mad, instead of glad, to see my best friend. I was mad when I saw the lines time had drawn on her face and the waves of her hair now almost completely white. Don't know how she could've stayed away so long. After we hugged she had to ask me if I was planning to let her in. Part of me wanted to say "Naw, go on back where you came from." You know that wasn't nothing but the devil either.

We spent the afternoon laughing and talking about old times. Priscilla couldn't remember any of our classmates—then again why would she.

By nightfall I'd showed her to the guest room. She unpacked, put on her sleeping clothes and joined me on the porch. We sat silently for a long time. Priscilla said it'd been years since she'd heard crickets cuz there were no crickets in New York City. It felt good sitting next to my old friend. For the first time in ages I didn't miss Lee. Before I knew anything I'd reached out to hold her hand. As I did it, I realized I'd never held her hand all the years we'd known each other. It was something different about holding her hand. It wasn't like holding my childrens' hands to keep them from running off and harming themselves or like holding Lee's hand when we went for walks after church on Sunday. We sat there—quietly for the most part, chuckling every once in awhile when the crickets seemed to be getting beside themselves.

I told Priscilla I had an old, old bottle of Lee's Mogen David wine under the kitchen sink and if she was interested we could have a night cap. I'd read in *The Ladies Home Journal* that high class people often enjoy a night cap before going to bed. I apologized for the cheapness of the wine. Priscilla told me to hush up 'cuz it was a wonderful suggestion.

When I returned to the porch with the wine I pulled my rocker closer to hers. I was quiet for a spell but then that ole' devil got a hold of my tongue. He just wouldn't let me enjoy the moment. I asked Priscilla why she never paid any mind to all my letters begging her to visit. She told me she couldn't return because she'd lost something so dear to her in Tyler. When I asked her what she'd lost she didn't answer so I repeated myself.

She uncrossed her legs, placed both feet on the porch and stopped the rocker. "Leta, I lost you."

Then it hit me. I suddenly knew why Priscilla cut her hair as a child, why the boys stopped chasing her, why mama lied to her, and why the whole town stopped speaking. That ole devil told me I knew even more too. I knew why I wanted to cut my hair, why I loved looking at that scar, why I married Lee in such a hurry, and why I could never let myself leave Tyler to visit her.

I drew a long sip of wine from my glass decorated with faded, yellow flowers—I'd collected the whole set from the Piggly Wiggly. Thinking about all those lost years made even that sweet wine taste bitter. I reached out again for Priscilla's hand and this time she took hold of mine, gently. I looked out into the Texas night and said something I can't exactly blame on the devil. I said, "Well, now you've found me."

Conversation At Lucy's

"I remember exactly. You were wearing a white cotton shirt and khakis. You came in late, pulled your glasses off your face in very dramatic fashion and pulled up a chair."

"What else do you remember?"

"Well, let's see. I remember thinking she's really beautiful. Really beautiful."

"You did not think that."

"I did too. During the orientation I kept trying to make eye contact with you but you wouldn't look in my direction. I think you felt my eyes on you. You were trying to be cool."

"I probably was. I'd already set my sights on you."

"You're full of shit."

"No. Seriously, I had. I'd seen you walking around campus. I thought you were cute too. I know when I looked into your eyes upon our first introduction I felt pulled in so I tried to act engaged in something else."

"Yeah, the cool one."

"I don't know how cool I was. I showed up for our first

study session with a picnic basket didn't I?"

"Yes—with German chocolate, strawberries, chicken salad, fresh baked french bread and fancy mineral water in a blue bottle."

"I was playing Casanova."

"Hardly. Do you remember what you said when I commented on the picnic basket?"

"No. Not really."

"You said—you poor thing, I guess you think this is a date."

"Well, I only said that because I really liked you."

"Really?"

"Really. You know, I go crazy when you look at me like that."

"Like what?"

"Like that. Oh, and now you're using the voice."

"What voice babe?"

"That voice."

"So, what do you think of this place?"

"I think I'm lucky to have a girlfriend smart enough to ask a local where the gay-owned establishments are. This is a gem of a spot and in Rhode Island. I never would've guessed it. I am glad we're vacationing. I can't wait to get to the Cape tomorrow."

"Is that all?"

"Well, you cut me off. Lemme finish. I am glad, I am truly glad you came into my life. I like seeing the world through your eyes. I like learning with you. For the first time in longer than I care to admit I don't want to be anyplace else. I am in love with this moment and in love with you—so much that I am committed to doing whatever it takes to have more moments like this one."

"Well, let me make a final toast."

"How many times have we toasted?"

"Shh—it doesn't matter. Can I make another toast?"

"Please do."

"To us. One year down, a lifetime to go."

"You're giving me that look again."

"What look?"

"Oh come on, don't be coy."

"Should I ask for the check now?"

"Please do."

When Sunny Gets Blue*

I seen it. Seen it when it walked through the door. Come for her. Big and bad as it wanna be. Death. I tell her, "Fight it baby. Fight it. Hold on to your life." But she just take Mr. Death by the hand. Escort him to our bed.

We had an old love. Our love had an old feeling to it—a strong familiarity, a kind of sacred knowing. I felt like I loved her since before Jesus's time. Here's our story.

She was named after a tune or that big ball of yellow in the sky, my Sunny. Met her when I was just a young thing. Selling magazine subscriptions, make-up, or knives—selling something door-to-door that summer to buy books that fall semester—my second year in college.

I come upon the last house on Belton Boulevard. On my way to this strange front door I feel like I'm going home. The house looks old. I expect the stairs to squeak as I travel them. They don't. The screen door's half open—even in times like these? I ask myself. Trusting soul. My mind tells my hand to knock but before I can she appears in a yellow dress.

"Hi hon."

She don't even know me, calling me hon. But I like it so I don't correct her. Naw, I smile back 'cause she greeted me with a smile. I say "helloow." Don't mean for my voice to come out thick as wet sand but it's hot outside and I'm tired. I pitch her the sale for magazine subscriptions, make-up, knives or whatever I'm selling. She say she'll buy, but come in from the pouring sun. Most of the folks in this neighborhood can't even afford fans—they sitting out on their porches and I sell to them there. Them same folks got squeaky stairs too. Should've know Sunny was different. Her stairs didn't squeak. I go in. Sold her something. Went on my way.

"Hush your crying hon. It'll be all right. You'll be fine. Come on now...hush. Hush. You gon' make me wish I'd never told you."

Don't know why I delivered her product first. Funny, I still can't tell you what it was that I was selling or what she bought. But I remember she was forty-six or forty-seven on my list. I walked to her house first. Didn't bother with calling. Figured it wouldn't be a waste even if I just got to see the house.

"You'll be fine. Don't you know I'll always be with you. Always. Come on. Hush now. Don't make Mr. Death mad. He'll come back early for you and we don't want that happening. You have so much work to do. So much work. My work on this side is done. Come here. Lay beside me. Hold my hand."

When I turned onto her block I heard music coming from her door:

> When Sunny gets blue
> her eyes get gray and cloudy
> then the rain begins to fall.
> Pitter patter. Pitter patter.
> Love is gone so what can matter.
> No sweet lover man comes to call—

My feet carry me to the rhythm of the drumsong beating itself out inside my chest. The sidewalk feels like burning sand. Blisters will form on the soles of my feet if I don't get there soon enough. Never mind I'm wearing new shoes. The music gets louder:

> When Sunny gets blue
> she breathes a sigh of sadness
> like the wind that disturbs the tress.
> Winds that set the leaves swayin'
> like some violins playin'
> weird and haunting melodies—

My drumsong gets even louder. I'm no longer walking. I know this because whatever I am selling is swinging in my arm. So, I must be running.

People used to love
to see her smile,
hear her laugh
that's how she got her name.
Since that sad affair,
she's lost her smile,
changed her style.
Somehow, she's not
not the same.

My drumsong stops. Walking up her stairs, questions fill me—fill me like the sun. Who is this woman?

She appears again. "Hello hon. Well, you said a couple of weeks. I love a person that keeps her word. Look at you sweating. Come in. I'm steaping sun-tea on the back porch." A smile flashes at me.

But memories will fade.
And pretty dreams will rise up,
where her other dreams fell through.
Hurry, hurry, hurry new love here
to kiss away each lonely tear
and hold her near
when Sunny gets blue.*

---

* "When Sunny Gets Blue" was written and composed in 1956 by Jack Segal and Marvin Fisher.

She pours me a glass of sun-tea on the song's last note.

"I was named for that song or that light and heat-giving source," she starts telling me. "Depends on which parent of mine you're considering. Mama was a sad person. Loved the blues—only an occasional jazz tune and only if it had a melancholy feel to it. She hated 'swing.' Called it happy music. Now Daddy, my daddy was a happy man. Too happy to stay at home. Funny how when she used to call my name I felt like the rain. When Daddy called me I knew I was the light in his life. Tell me the story of your name."

Mr. Death experienced this enough to know the person dying need enough time to impart wisdom and love. With this knowing he stands guard with a deaf ear to my prayers for more time. "Hush up now. I need you to hear me and hear me good. Remember every story I told you. Remember me. Remember every goal, every dream you had in this house. Remember the love, our love and share it with others because this journey ain't always easy—most times it's hard. Giving and receiving love is what makes it bearable. Remember our love. Pass it on."

Started dropping by Sunny's between classes for a story, a glass of sun-tea, sometimes a sandwich and always a smile. Always. It was the stories that helped me to love her. She made owning up to your mistakes sound so easy. She made loving and forgiving most enticing. During those days I didn't talk much.

She was okay with that. I told her once that I felt bad coming to her house all the time getting her stories and her food for free. "You don't feel bad or else you wouldn't do it. Besides..." she went on, "you give me gifts too but it's not my place to tell you what they are. You've got to learn for yourself what you possess so no one can tell you what you do or don't have."

When the weather got bad Sunny would come to the dormitory to pick me up. She drove a blue Cadillac. The fleetwood model. On rainy or snowy days we'd go back to her house. While she sewed, she'd talk me through a chilli, stew or soup recipe. I was always instructed to take the leftovers home for the other girls in my dorm who "might crave something after the dinning hall closed."

By the time spring and our second summer knowing each other rolled around I'd found my gifts—some of them—and started sharing them with Sunny. The sharing was easy—easier than it'd ever been in my childhood home. You fall in love when the sharing is that easy. Do you hear me? You fall in love.

The folks in my family, who I was never that close to except my baby sister, commented on the new me. Blamed the added weight on the cafeteria food and the smile on God. They never thought to give love the credit. And my gifts—they never noticed them so I didn't share them.

I seen it. Seen it when it walked through the door. Didn't know he would stay. Didn't know she'd escort him in. Thought maybe he was bringing a message: Take care of yourself Sunny. Didn't know she wanted him to take her. How could she want to go? Didn't she love me too?

On some days there was no need for words or actions. I could just be. Sunny knew and taught me how to share in the silence. Sometimes the sharing got so intense I had to excuse myself from myself. When she reached out to hold me, I told my soul—pardon me. That was something between my soul's and Sunny's. At least, that was the way it was in the beginning when the sharing used to scare me. Towards the end, I'd learned to hold on to my soul and hers too.

"Do you remember the song that was playing the day you brought me that beautiful gift wrap I'd ordered from you? *When Sunny Gets Blue*—play it for me now. When I told you the story of my name that day, I knew one thing. I knew I had —in another time and place—loved you for as long as I have believed in Jesus. You are the only person I shared the story of my name with. Play the song again. Please. And, here. Come here. Let me hold you and tell you that story again."

I'm holding on to my Sunny. I'm holding on to my soul and hers too. I can't let go. I won't let go. I hold on even tighter as I feel life slip out of her body.

She's going

going

going…

By the song's last chord she is gone. I shout. Moan. Cry out. Because, I can't let go and I know I'll never be able to. A chill enters the room.

You don't let go of the memories. But you move on. You must move on.

"Julia, will you come to the market with me?"

"We don't need anything from the market," she snaps back.

"Of course we do baby. Tomorrow is Thanksgiving."

"Well, I'm not really into turkey Linda. You know that." The sharpness of her words slice the air in our bedroom.

I take another deep breath and try a different approach.

"What dishes did you eat at home on holidays? I mean, I know you didn't celebrate Thanksgiving in Trinidad but what would you typically eat for special occasions?"

Julia scrunches her nose and lips together formulating her pouty 'I'm thinking' expression. She comes back to the bed and collapses on it. Pulling the magenta down comforter over her head she softly says, "I miss callaloo." I am surprised by her admission. I reach under the comforter and take her in my arms before asking, "What is callaloo?"

"Callaloo develops from a West African idea of stewing greens down to a smooth puree," she begins.

Having been raised by my grandmother, a southern woman who loved vegetables, I am familiar with all types of greens—mustards, collards, kale and turnips. I smile remembering how I loved eating my grandmother's greens. The smile lingers as I realize Julia and I have this in common.

"Callaloo is the leaf of a taro plant," she explains. Silence begins to fill our bedroom and I know her mind has traveled back to Trinidad and memories of home. In effort to break the silence and bring her back to me I make a suggestion.

"Let's make callaloo."

"I don't have mam-maw's secret recipe. I never learned how to make it. All the women in my family learn to make it when they reach adulthood. I left home at seventeen—not yet an adult by mam-maw's standards."

"We'll find a recipe," I offer in my most promising tone.

Julia begins to cry. Then she sobs. Soon her nose is stuffy and her chest is heaving. This has been a long, long time coming. I hold her closer me and encourage this release.

After she is empty of tears and assured of my love for her, Julia and I get dressed bombarding each other with vivid stories from our family histories. We curse the memories of bullies and the firsts to break our hearts. We laugh during the especially funny stories of odd cousins and sibling rivalry. We offer condolences when stories of deceased childhood pets and lost friends are shared. Most importantly, we connect.

We drive to the nearest women's bookstore and begin our hunt for a callaloo recipe. We pull twenty cookbooks from the shelves and sit on the floor to begin our search. When she's looked through four or five cookbooks, Julia gives up. I know this by the way she forms a bridge with her hands and cracks her knuckles. Cracking her knuckles serves as her admission of failure. Just as she is about to say what I guess will be an 'oh well,' I turn a page and see:

I begin to read the recipe aloud while Julia crawls over to where I am sitting, squealing in delight.

Callaloo/Serves Four

1 pound fresh callaloo greens (Spinach may be substituted)

1 pound okra, topped & tailed

1 onion coarsely chopped

1 bouquet garni, prepared from scallions, fresh thyme, parsley
and chives

Salt & pepper to taste

1 clove garlic, minced

1/2 pound cooked ham, cut into 1/4 inch dice-sized portions

Juice of 2 limes.

We buy the cookbook and head for the market.

After Thanksgiving dinner, which includes callaloo, plan-
tains, curry chicken, chick peas and rice, cocobread, and other
favorite foods that leap from our childhood memories, Julia and
I make love. Though I know I have not filled Julia's void, I
believe we are both beginning to heal. I'm glad our home has
become the space where healing can occur. Julia sleeps.
Quietly, I inch closer to my lover in search of that perfect spot
to nuzzle between her neck and shoulder. She shifts a little and
speaks a few words I don't understand. I wrap my arm around
her.

Her half-asleep voice whispers, "In case you were wondering, those words mean I love you."

Afterword

In workshops I have given at women's prisons, women's music festivals and following many public readings, I have often encountered women possessed of a keen desire to further explore women's literature. While it has brought me much pleasure to offer book suggestions (I eagerly scribble down titles and their authors on any paper shoved in my direction), I find it even more exciting to take advantage of this time and space by paying homage to those women writers, past and present, who helped me to love reading and inspired me to pick up my pen time after time. May this list also inspire you!

LaShonda K. Barnett, June 1999

Dorothy Allison

Maya Angelou

Tina McElroy Ansa

Djuna Barnes

Aphra Behn

Sharon Bridgforth

Rita Mae Brown

Kate Chopin

Sandra Cisneros

Pearl Cleage

J. California Cooper

Edwidge Danticat

Lillian Faderman

Jessie Redmon Fauset

Jewelle Gomez

Radcliffe Hall

bell hooks

Gloria T. Hull

Zora Neale Hurston

Nella Larsen

Audre Lorde

Katherine Mansfield

Terry McMillan

Penny Mickelbury

Isabel Miller

Lisa C. Moore

Kathleen E. Morrir

Toni Morrison

Gloria Naylor

Lesléa Newman

Joan Nestle

Anäis Nin

Flannery O'Connor

Ann Petry

Jean Rhys

Sapphire

Ntozake Shange

Ann Allen Shockley

Kitty Tsui

A.J. Verdelle

Alice Walker

Mary Helen Washington

Harriet E. Wilson

Virginia Woolf

and

Shay Youngblood

For more about New Victoria Publishers Books
Call or Send for a Free Catalog

New Victoria Publishers
PO Box 27 Norwich, Vermont 05055
1 800 326 5297   1802 649 5297
Email: newvic@aol.com
Webpage: http://www.opendoor.com/NewVic/